The Ison Delusion

Published by David James Publishing 2013
Copyright © 2013 by Samantha J Wright

This book is a work of fiction and where appropriate names, characters, some places and incidents either are products of the author's imagination or are used fictitiously.

The right of Samantha J Wright to be identified as the author of this work has been asserted by him in accordance with the Copyright, Designs and Patents Act of 1988.

All rights reserved, including right to reproduce this book or portions thereof in any form whatsoever.

First David James Publishing edition 2013
www.davidjamespublishing.com

Cover Design: Samantha J Wright

A CIP catalogue record for this book is available from the British Library
ISBN: 978-09575610-4-5

Also by Samantha J Wright

Crossbreed 6
A Darker 6
Night Chorus
The Sands of Carsaig

For my children Ethan and Jessica,
my universe and my strength

The Ison Delusion

by

Samantha J Wright

PROLOGUE

CHRIS GAZED INTO the watery abyss and for the life of him could not think why he'd agreed to do this. Yet it had seemed like such a good idea at the time. He looked up at the sound of water falling in icy beads from the tips of calciferous stalactites on to the cave floor. They reminded him of snake fangs oozing deadly poison. That thought sent a shudder dancing across his shoulder blades. He suppressed it and strove to banish that analogy from his mind. He shouldn't be nervous, he told himself over and over. Every member of their six man team was an expert in their chosen field and they were all experienced divers.

Although neither he nor Ralph, the camera man, had ever set foot in a cave before, between the two of them they had clocked up hundreds of diving hours filming a documentary called *Sunken Treasures*.

That's why they were here in Krslja – to film another documentary that would hopefully raise their profile enough so that they could do a follow up series to the first. They were eager to return to those underwater ruins as soon as possible before the site was plundered – a common occurrence in the waters off southern Laconia. Central Croatia just didn't hold the same excitement for them as Greece. Still, it was a means to an end.

"You got the backup power cells for camera two Chris?" called Ralph. He was putting on his belt, the one with the floating guide line that would lead them back to safety when the time came.

"Yep, they're in my pocket," he answered slapping his leg. To make doubly sure they were kept dry he'd stashed the batteries in a waterproof compartment inside his dry suit.

A quick glance at the rest of the team told him that they too were busy making last minute checks. He tried to find reassurance in this.

"I think we are almost ready," rumbled Sven, towering over him.

"Ok," he nodded hoping he appeared more relaxed than he felt. "Let's do this."

Whilst he inflated his thick Permatek dry suit the others donned their neoprene balaclavas in readiness for the dive. These were designed to be worn beneath their helmets for extra protection from the cold. Only their ears, eyes, nose and mouth protruded from beneath the stretchy black fabric and they were soon to be covered by their lightweight helmets.

Once they were fully kitted out the men turned rather awkwardly to regard each other noting how much they resembled characters from a Jules Verne novel. Somehow Chris failed to see the funny side.

Gradually the headgear was pressurized until the read outs on the dials were equal. The only thing left now was a sound check which Simon, the ex-Navy Seal, performed as he was the head of the expedition.

"One, two, three. One, two, three. Thumbs up if you can hear me," he said sounding slightly breathless.

Everyone offered the required thumbs up apart from Dan who casually flipped a middle finger and grinned.

Simon ignored his behavior and slipped into the water to fasten himself to Sven his diving partner. Chris smirked knowing that Dan would be really pissed off now. He loved provoking a reaction. But Simon had obviously sized him up already and wasn't about to fall for any of that nonsense.

"Ok. Looks like we're good to go," he said. "Everyone remember the rules and keep close together."

Chris looked down dubiously, trying not to think about the dangers that lay ahead of them. Behind him Dan fastened their buddy tether and gave it a pull to test its reliability.

"Ok twin. Time to return to the womb," he laughed dropping feet first into the water.

Chris gulped painfully, his mouth felt uncomfortably dry. With a splash Ralph and Kurt jumped in, both of them treading water as they waited for him to join them.

A cold prickle of sweat broke out at the curve of his spine. He squeezed his eyes shut hoping that they could not sense his fear. Hell, they could probably hear his heart beat! he thought glumly.

His breath hitched low in his throat as he stepped off the rocky shelf, plunging into the freezing sink hole below. He gave a reflexive gasp, expecting the cold to hit him like a brick wall. When it didn't, a nervous little laugh escaped him.

"That wasn't so bad!" he admitted.

It felt odd being cocooned so completely. He was used to

the feel of the water on his skin; the gentle rock of the ocean and the sun beaming down from above.

Alongside the rest of the team he patiently bobbed up and down, awaiting Simon's signal. They watched as he gave one last check of the guideline's moorings then smoothly disappeared from view. Everyone else followed all except for Chris who hesitated, torn between wanting to do what he had set out to do and wanting to avoid dark enclosed spaces. A gentle tug on the tether urged him to follow. It could not be ignored. He was part of a team and no matter what his fears were he could not let them down. Bearing that in mind he gathered every ounce of professionalism he could muster and dived into the gloom with a purposeful kick of his flippers.

Immediately the rasp of his own breath filled his ears as he found himself in a world without warmth. It was nothing like diving in the Med. If that had been yang this was its yin. Ambient sound had been replaced by an unrelenting pressure. Blackness pressed in on every side reminding them that they were surrounded by enormous quantities of water and rock. Fear and a creeping chill strove to hold them captive. They were not easy assailants to overthrow. Chris's limbs felt heavy as though he'd become a fetus encased within a womb of stone and yet beside him his allegorical twin, Dan, seemed unaffected.

He swam after the others, following the dim yet comforting glow of their lights until his powerful strokes left the line between them taut.

"You ok?" said his voice, filtering through Chris's earpiece.

"Just a little claustrophobic."

"Is that all?" chuckled Dan.

"Yeah, that and it's bloody cold!"

He waited for the mocking to begin but the insults never came. Maybe he was suffering from a mild attack of empathy.

The group swam on and on, turning this way and that. Occasionally one of them banged an elbow or knee off the rock.

Better be careful, thought Chris. If someone gets a puncture in their suit they could end up with the bends or worse.

At one point the tunnel narrowed so much they could feel their tanks bumping along the roof. This unnerved him so he slowed down heedless of the fact he was falling behind. He preferred to take his time and live thank you very much!

Once past the especially narrow part he kicked vigorously in order to catch up. He was beginning to feel like a car stuck in a queue of traffic – continuous pausing preventing it from making much headway.

These damn cave paintings had better be worth it, he thought irritably.

Just how they were going to find their way out even with the help of the guide line was beyond him. It was so dark and they had travelled so far. Diving in the warm waters of the Med had spoiled him. This experience was something else entirely. All he could do to combat his fears was focus on following the rest of the team.

You're not alone! You're not alone! became his own personal mantra.

It helped ward of the irrational fear that something was stalking him, lurking in the bottomless depths.

At least it did until something unexpectedly touched him.

"Fuck!"

Everyone came to an abrupt halt.

"What's up?" said Simon calmly. Chris finally saw why Dan found him so irritating.

"Something just touched me!" he blurted out.

"It was probably just a fish or an air bubble. Not that unusual, especially prior to seismic activity."

"Please tell me you're joking," said Dan. He sounded a little tense.

"Don't worry," Simon answered breezily. "I already checked the seismic activity in the area. Barely a blip for months on end. As for fish, there's probably nothing bigger than a mackerel in here. Not enough ecosystem to support it."

"So it was probably just a cave shrimp fart, buddy," said Dan with a grin in his voice. The opportunity to have fun at Chris's expense was too good to pass up.

"Huh! Well don't say I didn't warn you," grumbled Chris. "For all you know we could be sharing this cave with Jaws."

"More like Moby *Dick*!" chuckled Dan.

"Who are you calling a dick?" snapped Chris, purposefully shining his headlamp into the other man's eyes. Dan had never had been a very tactful man.

"Hey! We're wasting valuable oxygen here," said Simon tapping or rather touching them both on the shoulder. "Time to move on."

Wounded pride held them back from answering. Ignorant bastard! I'm paying his goddamn wages, thought Chris as they resumed the dive. He boiled for a bit but in some dark straight talking corner of his mind a remnant of common sense wagged its finger. He knew Simon was right. They had far more important things to do right now. Their lives depended on being able to think clearly.

Ten minutes later Chris got the impression they were starting to rise as though about to surface. But it was hard to tell for certain as no natural light could reach that far down. He was impatient to find out, so he picked up the pace overtaking Dan his companion. He wanted filming down here over and done with so that they could return to their safe, comfy hotel in Talac – a sleepy little town stuck in a time warp at the foot of the Croatian mountains. He was looking forward to sampling a few pints of the local brew there later.

A few seconds later they surfaced inside a colossal cavern. Disoriented they looked up into the artificial night, feeling insignificant and small like a bunch of amoebas floating in a dirty puddle. It was Chris, ever the reflective one who wondered about the man who'd originally discovered the place thinking that it must have taken some guts to go it alone - either that or a death wish. He made a mental note to find out more about him the moment he got back to his hotel.

Sven was the first to haul out. While the others followed suit he snapped a number of glow sticks so that they made a brittle cracking sound then handed them out like a giant Father Christmas. Behind him Simon swept a powerful flash light in a wide arc laying bare everything its beam touched. Beneath its brilliance huge swathes of crystals glittered like stars in the night. The men looked up and blinked, startled by its beauty.

"Wow! Are you getting all this Ralph?" exclaimed Chris.
"Yep."

He was aiming the camera with surprisingly steady hands

considering they'd only just gotten out of the water. Chris on the other hand was not quite so hardy. The cold had gotten into his bones and he couldn't keep still for shivering. The only answer was to move around.

"So where are these cave drawings then?" he asked Kurt. He was their main researcher.

"Your guess is as good as mine," he answered. "The guy who found them died in 1999. The only information left to us was in his journals. But they're pretty vague. The best thing we can do is spread out."

After twenty minutes of careful searching they found them beneath a sloping overhang, partially shielded by a rock fall. They were ancient and amazingly detailed.

As with many paintings of their kind the predominant theme was of the hunt. Human males carried upright spears or sharpened poles and some ran to herd their quarry towards the others. Antelope and cattle with monstrous curved horns roamed the plains. Some had grass in their mouth, others had young by their side. The scenes were so animated they felt themselves transported to the artists time. It was extraordinary.

Further along the wall pendulous breasted women tended fires and prepared food. Another scene depicted the entire tribe dancing naked beneath a full moon.

The group stood in silence as Ralph captured the whole thing on film.

"Oh my GOD! You have got to come and see this!" someone shouted.

It was Dan. He was right at the back of the cave having wandered there once he lost interest in the drawings.

Understandably curious, they followed and were surprised to see a small tunnel leading to a secondary cavern. In order to reach it they would have to crawl on their hands and knees. This posed a serious risk to the integrity of their suits. Ralph assured them that it was worth it.

"What is it?" asked Kurt.

"You're not going to believe it…" he told them over his shoulder. Shivers ran up and down Chris's spine in anticipation of what he'd discovered. An air of expectancy hung between them. The echo of history was powerful in these caves.

After a minute or two of awkward shuffling they found themselves standing in a second chamber. Only this one was tiny in comparison to the one they had just left. It appeared smaller still due to the huge raised platform standing in the center. Any bigger and it would have filled the room.

However the size of the pitted limestone slab was not what interested them. It was what lay upon it that had grabbed their attention - a very old, complete human skeleton. The bones were almost black with age and liberally peppered with miniscule holes. From the shape of the pelvic bones they judged her to be a female who had lived to a ripe old age and had suffered from severe osteoporosis for some time. The significance of this unexpected find made Chris's legs go weak. He sat down on a boulder and listened to the others talk amongst themselves.

"Geological evidence indicates that a hundred and fifty thousand years have passed since these caves were last exposed. Do you realize what that means? This could well be the mother of modern man," breathed Ralph through the intercom. Everyone nodded.

"Whoever she was she must have been very special to be interred inside the tribal cave. I've never heard of such a thing," said Sven.

"How has it even survived? I know it's in a sealed environment and everything but even so this shouldn't be possible," said Dan.

"Look…I hate to be a spoil sport here…" began Simon.

"Shh…" scolded Chris holding up a finger. If he hadn't been so enthralled by what he had spotted he might have seen Dan's delight at the curtailment of Simon's speech. Instead he pointed over at the wall behind the skeletons head.

"What is that?" exclaimed Ralph zooming in to film the unusual symbols.

"I have no idea. Look! There's another one behind us," said Dan.

"This one's very different though," someone pointed out.
Look, I really must insist that we go now. We have spent long enough down here," interrupted Simon. "We need to give ourselves plenty of time to get back."

At the very mention of the return journey Chris's heart sank. He did not know if he could do it all over again no matter how stupendous their discovery. Just in case he could not return he decided he must take a bone sample so that he'd have something to carbon date.

"You guys go on ahead. I'll be with you in a minute," he told them.

"We must all stick together," Simon protested.

"I won't be long. I just want a bone sample from Granny here. Just a couple of minutes are all I need."

"Ok. We'll wait for you at the ledge in the main chamber."

As soon as they had disappeared into the tunnel leaving him alone, Chris grinned and fished out a sample bag from his breast pocket. He'd brought along a pair of tweezers too – just in case. Experience had taught him to be prepared. He pulled open the bag using the tabs on either side and leaned forward to grab a piece of rib bone that had fallen onto the stone slab.

"It's ok Granny, this won't hurt a bit," he told her blithely. It was only later that he realized how wrong that statement was.

The moment he touched the bone a huge earthquake abruptly tore through the region raining down masses of stone throughout the caverns. The noise was thunderous with each jolt more powerful than the first. Everyone cried out in terror – even Simon. Wave after wave of tremors rattled and shook the place, knocking the men clean off their feet. Finally it stopped and the dust settled, revealing hundreds of tons of rock lying between Chris and the others. His worst nightmare had come true. He was trapped; no way in, no way out.

Just as he was thinking the situation couldn't get any worse a piece of limestone fell from the roof and caught him a glancing blow to the head. Their helmets were of light construction and were not designed to withstand such treatment. He slumped to the floor beside the skeletal remains, blood streaming everywhere like syrup from a maple tree. He ignored it, choosing to yell into the intercom instead.

"Simon! Can you hear me?"

After a brief pause he heard a voice.

"This is Ralph. Simon is dead."

"Shit! Ralph, you've got to get everyone out! Do it now

before there's another cave in!"

"We can't leave you behind."

"You've no choice. There's no way in or out. I'm trapped here for good. Save yourselves. It's up to you to tell the people what we've found."

There was a pause.

"Ok," said Ralph reluctantly. "Do you want me to carry a message to anyone?"

"Yeah. Tell my dog, Cooper, that I love him and see that he finds a good home."

"Ok."

Chris could almost see him struggling to do what he knew he had to.

"It's been a privilege working with you Ralph. You're a good guy. But it's time to go."

"You too Chris. I…" suddenly he was interrupted by another huge tremor. It was as though the cavern wanted to rid itself of their presence.

"GO Ralph! GO!"

"Ok. We're going. Be strong Chris…" And that was the last he heard of them.

What with his head wound and the shaking, his insides were doing a pretty good imitation of a cement mixer. Eventually he was left with no choice but to remove his helmet and vomit into the stale death laden air. He found it just about breathable but for what little time he had left he preferred the clean air from his tank.

As he fastened the last catch on his helmet a light headed acceptance of his fate flooded his consciousness. Fear and worry left him like swallows on the wing. Strangely although trapped, he had never felt freer in his life. He had no need to worry about tomorrow or the next day. There simply wasn't going to be a next day. Not for him.

Instead he rested his head against the frigid unyielding stone, gazing up at the extraordinary relief that had been painted so long ago. Now that the earth had stilled once more he felt he should use whatever time he had left to see if he could figure out its meaning. Better that than give in to fear.

The central image was of a snake eating itself – which thousands of years after the artist had originally painted it would later become known as the *ouroboros* symbol; the universal symbol of cyclicality. Inside that circle were four other images: a primitive looking bird with a twig in its mouth, the sun, something that looked like a fruit or an egg and finally a triangular snowcapped mountain. The whole thing was surrounded by hundreds and hundreds of concentric circles drawn around the main image. At the bottom a young woman with piercing eyes looked directly at him with her knees drawn up and her arms draped loosely across them.

He stared and stared, trying to figure it out until finally he lost consciousness. A while later he awoke again to find that the light was getting dimmer and that blood loss had robbed him of his strength. It all felt extremely surreal. Especially the paintings. What could they mean, he wondered?

He began to think about the snake symbol and how the four things depicted inside it perhaps represented a cycle of some sort. With nothing else to do he puzzled and puzzled over it to the point where he made himself dizzy, until all of a sudden it came to him! Finally he understood what he was looking at - it was a calendar!

The bird with a twig symbolized spring – the time when most birds build their nests. The sun represented summer. The fruit represented autumn, the time when many berries and fruits are ripe for gathering. And the snowy mountain, crude as it was represented winter.

So what did the three hundred and six lines mean that had been drawn around the *ouroboros* symbol? It seemed logical that they were years but they were surely not the years of life that this woman had lived. It was simply not possible to live that long.

Her eyes bored into him from across the room as though in contradiction. He stared back wishing she could speak. Time was running out.

Her eyes really did seem to be trained on him. Or were they? Could it be that she was staring at something else?

He scrambled across the room on his hands and knees only to discover that like him she was gazing at an image on the opposite wall. Only this one was very different.

Against a dry and dusty looking landscape four little figures were disappearing over the horizon. Above them in what had to be the brightest paint these people could create someone had daubed a magnificent comet blazing across the sky. It outshone everything else in the sky; all the stars, even the moon.

The magnitude of what his team had discovered swelled like a spring tide within him. Before him on those uneven walls was the very first recorded instance of a comet and the first known calendar! It was truly an amazing discovery – the absolute highlight of his career, the pinnacle of all his achievements. He smiled and wiped away a tear, thinking just how proud his mother would have been if only she was still alive.

As the light diminished and the last of his air faded away he made a concerted effort not to focus on the twisted irony. Instead he reached out and took the hand of the skeleton feeling the roughness of her bones against his now bare palm. Leaning forward he thanked her for sharing her secret and together they took one last look at the mighty comet. He laid his carcass down and with trembling fingers removed his now useless helmet.

"What goes around comes around," he told his companion of the labyrinth.

Two seconds later death reached out and took him. The moment it did so the chamber imploded.

Chapter One

The Mark

THE LAST OF the fading sunlight was all but gone leaving a dull orange glow across the under belly of the sky. I got the impression that the city was more than ready for the night after the scorching ninety degree heat of the day. Close by a faint click signalled the opening of a car door, its gleaming metallic paintwork reflecting all that remained of a dazzling sunset.

Quietly I lay in wait feeling nervous yet keen to see the monster whose file I'd been perusing for days. I silently wondered if he would live up to his reputation.

Suddenly there he was, framed in the car doorway – all six foot three inches of him.

I'd like to have been able to say that his ugliness was breath taking. It would have made much more sense to me somehow. But that would have been a gross exaggeration if not a down right lie. Sometimes the truth can be most inconvenient.

Instead the mark was a walking and talking Latino Adonis - dark haired with narrow rich brown eyes, the kind that flickered suspiciously over his surroundings. This told me two things. That he possessed intelligence and that he did not trust easily. Only intelligent people learn to question everything. That was at least two of my assumptions up in smoke already.

His skin was mocha coloured bordering on swarthy - what some people would mistakenly describe as half cast. To look at him you would think that there was something else in the mix – maybe Brazilian or Indonesian perhaps. He had that sort of look about him – a kind of melting pot of exotic features that came from somewhere within the neighboured of the equator. Why these things stood out to me I do not know. Perhaps I was imprinting the details of him on my mind to flesh out my otherwise sparsely furnished memory.

The file had described him as an intimidating character and it was easy to see why. His well-developed musculature was as prominent as his jailhouse tattoos, whose over-riding theme was anarchy. They intimated an unhealthy preoccupation with sex and death to the extent that if I'd had family, I wouldn't have wanted this man within a hundred miles of them. Casey was bad news indeed.

He stepped out of the vehicle with that lazy gangster stride of his, reeking of unspoken arrogance and menace, not to mention the invincibility he felt after snorting several lines of coke in the back seat. The car door slammed shut with an air of finality which wafted away the microscopic specks of gutter glitter that had lodged amongst the fibres of his clothes. I waited for him to leave but it appeared that they were not done yet. Someone inside was opening a window, as smooth as silk and as steady as molasses.

The windows were tinted inky black so that no one on the

outside could see in. It was perfect for concealing an SUV full of hoods and hoes from the watchful eye of justice…or so they presumed. With exaggerated casualness Casey leaned through the open passenger side window, to bump fists with the two joint smoking hoods sitting up front. This brief display was supposed to signify camaraderie and friendship. But I could see it was false. A momentary striking together of fists and it was gone. Theirs was a dog eat dog world and no matter how many times they grazed knuckles under the guise of brotherhood that fact still remained.

I knew there were others sitting in the back there. I could sense them rather than see them. They too probably liked to call themselves his friends but I suspect they were little more than acquaintances of his, serving a purpose and filling a need. Just like him their main focus was drugs and right next to that was their obsession for bling and designer gear. As much as possible they wanted to preen and strut like the stars they idolised. When they hadn't the energy or finances for either, they luxuriated on the back seat of their SUV like overfed cats reclining on a warm saggy sofa.

Unknown to them that security blanket lifestyle that they derived so much pleasure from had a great big gaping hole straight through the middle. Fun as it was their lifestyle was dangerous. Most of them would be lucky to make it past forty, by my reckoning.

By now Casey was flying high on the powdery white wings of euphoria. He felt good. He felt strong – maybe even a bit godlike. Not even the slight trickle of blood coming from his coke ravaged nose was enough to slow him down. He sniffed hard and thumbed it away as he moseyed off down the street like he owned the place.

I watched him go, deciding that this man was utterly disgusting. I felt repulsed with every fibre of my being because I knew of every shattered bone, sliced artery and broken heart he'd left behind in the deadly wake that followed his passing. In this instance it would be a pleasure for me to do my duty. I could hardly wait for that time to arrive.

He continued on his way casually sliding his hand up inside his jacket, checking for the cold hard touch of his newly acquired Beretta. Upon finding it there he smiled contentedly. That was something he could trust – up to a point. Aim and fire. What could be easier than that?

As with anything there was always the odd occasion when things went awry. So just in case, the Beretta was not the only weapon he carried. Men like him always carry backup, tucked away just in case the first failed or got lost in the heat of confrontation. His was in the back pocket of his jeans - a switch blade of tempered steel that he liked to brandish in front of people's faces whenever they crossed the line.

All this was in the file I'd been given along with the exact date and time I was supposed to take him down.

As much as I was glad of what was in the file I couldn't help feeling as though I needed a little more. It was just too selective for my liking. All the hours I had spent poring over it, looking for the whys and wherefores had not yielded the answers I desired.

I knew why him but I also needed to know, why now? Why not before? Hadn't enough people died already at Casey's hands?

It was difficult not to question why the boss had not already intervened when faced with the knowledge that another life was about to be taken. I felt I was missing something here.

An individual of his reputation had to have his reasons. But what they were remained a complete mystery. The boss knew what was about to go down tonight and how many other murders Casey Davenport had committed. Yet he still insisted that there was a much bigger picture, one that I was yet to discover. Try as I might I was damned if I could see it. I wanted to act *now*, before he struck again. This watch and wait stance was just too frustrating and in my humble opinion it was just plain wrong.

Admittedly it was futile wanting what I couldn't have – childish even. Full discretion to act whenever and in whatever way you saw fit was not a privilege you earned in five minutes. It took patience and dedication to the job. I needed to focus.

I followed him effortlessly like a lioness stalking a gazelle. I made no sound. Even the late evening shadows had more presence than I. I smiled to myself, pleased in the knowledge that my training was so far paying off.

We were moving into a smarter area now, one where trees lined the streets and the houses had sparkling blue swimming pools and electric gates. This was where the money was. Only the rich and privileged could afford to live like this. He was well on the way to sniffing out his next victim.

Beneath the steady glow of the many street lights a young woman towed along a miniature schnauzer as she headed confidently in our direction. It was the time of day when people were settling down to their evening meal and catching up on the latest news. The streets weren't exactly deserted but they weren't far off. This suited him well as he wanted to avoid attention.

The little dog looks peeved about being dragged along on the enforced route march. He dragged his heels wanting to stop and sniff but his Lycra clad mistress wouldn't allow it. Her jog through the leafy suburbs took precedent.

To Casey's delight the woman was the type that jogs with the determined enthusiasm of someone who doesn't really intend going that far – which was probably a wise move given the hour. Typical of so many in her generation she appeared to feel the need to be constantly entertained no matter where she was or what she was doing. On this occasion marshmallow earphones were feeding music directly into her ears drowning out all other distractions. Casey therefore felt quite safe in verbalising his approval of her toned physique and he did so the moment she passed by.

"That's the finest pair of tits and ass I've seen all day!" he grinned, staring after her.

She jogged on, pounding the pavement with her pricey Nikes, utterly oblivious to his crude observations. I tensed, half afraid of what this sexually predatory attitude would lead to. He had no such reservations.

From his perspective, everything was going swimmingly. Being in a well to do area was already having its advantages but as with everything there was a down side or a potential one at any rate. The trouble was he looked well out of place and smart as he was he knew it.

As much as he wanted to hang around and enjoy the view there was simply not enough time. He needed to act fast or split. Deeply ingrained survival instincts prompted him to turn away and pick up the pace until we came to a particularly imposing looking house. A concrete wall ran all the way round it at least eight feet high. At the gated entrance cameras rolled twenty four hours a day. As if that wasn't enough, several eye level signs warn that there were guard dogs on patrol. I secretly hoped that they were rabid Doberman Pinschers that hadn't been fed for a week. But based on what I knew of him I speculated that even that probably wouldn't be enough to keep out a determined felon of his calibre – especially when doped up to the eyeballs. Yet some ridiculously optimistic part of me still clung onto the hope that the possibility might be enough to make him have second thoughts.

All I could do was watch and wait, hoping he might see sense. I could see him carefully weighing up the options.

After a quick glance round he decided to rise to the challenge - quite literally thanks to a colourful maple tree with low twisted boughs hanging conveniently over the perimeter wall.

With cat like agility that I couldn't help but admire, he climbed the tree then jumped down into the shrubbery on the other side. In the stillness of the night he could be heard muttering curses into the velvety darkness. Apparently he didn't much like getting his hands dirty.

Apart from that all was quiet. There were no cars on the drive way and no lights were visible, save for those illuminating the exterior. The place looked empty. If only, I thought wistfully.

All I could do was follow at a distance, trying to resist the urge to dwell upon the injustice of it all. I just had to try to ignore the fact that we knew a murder was about to take place and that the big man upstairs was quite happy to sit back and do nothing.

I told myself it would do no good getting worked up about it. Best just get on with the job and play the hand I'd been dealt. If they could live with it then I had no choice but to try and do the same. *Who am I kidding?* I asked myself. Now *there*'s a question!

Whilst preoccupied with both delivering and listening to my own pep talk Casey scurried across the lush, well watered grass. Hastily he used whatever he could by way of cover – a fountain, a tree, whatever was handy.

All the while I was fervently hoping that someone would spot him and put an end to his nocturnal trespassing. Or that maybe those rabid, half-starved Doberman Pinschers would appear. My hopes were soon dashed. True to form he carried on unimpeded while hopelessness and frustration overwhelmed me. Someone must surely intervene before it was too late.

Once in the vicinity of the house itself, he found a downstairs window ajar. I almost cursed out loud. There was an open invitation if ever there was one. Why don't people heed the advice they're given? Leaving a ground floor window open is almost as bad as leaving a door open – a real no, no in the city.

Reaching in, he pushed it open wider still then climbed through into the study like a panther. Once inside his street smarts told him to avoid the safe. That would take too much time. What he really needed were valuables that would fuel his drug habit. So he went off in search of the bedrooms. They were a much more likely prospect.

Up the stairs, along the corridors he crept soft footed and hungry. Hungry for his next hit before he'd even swan dived from the pinnacle of the last. Instead of valuables he found a woman called Valentina Ostovell cleaning her employer's bedroom. This was not an entirely unexpected discovery. But my heart sank regardless.

"On the bed bitch!" he shouted, striding in.

She shrieked loudly at the sheer terror of being confronted by an intruder.

"Please! Please sir! I'm just the housekeeper!" she cried, backing away.

"Sit the fuck down. NOW!" he yelled, shoving the Beretta in her face.

Looking down the barrel of a gun she had no choice but to hastily comply. Her knees shook wildly as she stared at them ashen faced, trying to will herself to remain calm. Her life depended on it. She could feel it. This man meant business.

"Where are the goods? Jewellery and shit," he demanded, waving the gun around the luxurious room.

"I don't know." She really did look petrified.

"EH, EH!" he warned, making a sound exactly like a game show buzzer. "Wrong answer."

Suddenly he punched her in the face with enough force to break her nose. She sobbed and begged for mercy, choking on her own blood and tears. Roughly he pulled her to him by the hair, his eyes wild with ecstasy at the power he wielded over her.

It was impossible to watch. I felt sick. I couldn't stand it anymore. I knew exactly where this was going and I'd had enough. It was time to speak to the boss again. There had to be something I could do or say that would change his mind. So I crossed over into the fifth dimension and climbed the stairway to heaven...

Chapter Two

The Chat

"I'M HERE TO speak with God," I told the angel guarding the door.

He laughed at my ignorant presumption.

"God's kinda busy right now," he said, in a disturbing approximation of a Brooklyn accent.

"Yeah, well this is really important."

Unperturbed I stood my ground and straighten my slim black tie.

Let the battle of wills commence!

"So is his Saturday night card game," shrugged the burly angel, blocking the entrance with his huge sweaty bulk.

Craning over his shoulder I snuck a peek through the doorway but pink smoke (the type that certain night clubs use) billowed out obscuring my view. There was a peal of laughter from within followed by the sound of a chair over turning.

I couldn't decide which was more annoying, the angel or the laughter.

"Look. Just tell him Karma is here to see him," I growled. My patience was worn thin enough already without having to deal with this buffoon.

The angel looked at me uneasily, his Adam's apple jumping up and down like a cricket on Amphetamines. He seemed to be having a rethink.

"Wait here," he said dryly.

He ducked through the doorway and disappeared into the pink smoke. Within seconds he was back again.

"God will see you now," he said, motioning for me to go through. "But you'd better make it quick."

I found him sitting around a table along with several others where a weird looking card game was in progress.

"I see your fifty thousand souls and I raise you eleven hundred," he smiled, pushing a bunch of luminescent blue chips into the centre of the table.

"Come on Nick, what you got?" he grinned, elbowing the fiery looking gentleman to his left.

Nick gazed thoughtfully at his cards, his expression inscrutable. I was deeply disturbed to see it was no ordinary deck that they were playing with. The kings, queens and jacks were the rulers and big players of the world and the numbers were the ordinary folk - the masses.

"Karma!" God cried, as if he's only just noticed me. "What are you doing here? I thought you were away on business?"

Inside I bristled with rage at his detachment from what was going on down below but I had no choice but to keep it together.

"I had to come back – try to convince you that Valentina deserves to be saved. It's no good waiting till he's raped and killed her then swooping in. She needs our help – now," I urged him. Ironically it felt awkward asking God for favours. *Wasn't that what people were supposed to do?*

I looked down at the table and saw Valentina's face on the seven of clubs, one of the many cards God held in his hand.

"Karma, Karma, Karma..." he sighed, leaning his head on one side. "It's no good getting emotional where these humans are concerned. I know you don't agree, but this way really is the best. We can't save them all. But every now and then YOU, my dear friend, can teach them an important lesson they won't forget in a hurry. And that's what's due to happen to Casey Davenport in about twenty two minutes from now."

He looked at his watch briefly then turned his attention back to his cards.

Dear friend? Since when was I his dear friend? This was news to me!

"Why? Why can't we save them all? Why do any of them have to die?" I asked, already knowing my questions were pointless. *After all, God knew everything. Didn't he?*

"Listen to yourself. Listen to the childishness of what you are suggesting Karma. Imagine a world where no one dies, gets ill, or commits crime. Who would bother going to the churches, mosques, temples and synagogues? Who would pray? What would be the point?" God said gravely.

The authority he projected with just his voice alone was incredible. It was hard not to succumb to its influence.

"But on the other hand why should they pray to you anyway when you repeatedly ignore their suffering and only intervene when it suits your purposes?" I objected bitterly.

"Show some respect!" the angel boomed. He stepped forward as though about to unsheathe his sword. Defenceless, I shielded my face and head with my hands

"Now, now," God commanded, waving him back. "No need for that."

"His kind don't belong here!" the angel rumbled.

What did he mean by that?

God chose to ignore him and looked at me thoughtfully for a minute or two.

"Perhaps I've made a mistake in giving you the position of Karma," he mused, rubbing his pure white goatee beard. "Maybe it's not quite right for you. I suppose I could have a word with superhuman resources and see what other jobs opportunities are open to you. How does that sound?"

"It's ok," I insisted, realising that I was getting nowhere. I might end up with an even worse job at this rate! "I've got this. I know what my duties are. I just needed some clarification."

I could hear Nick snickering under his breath.

"Maybe you should read the bible then," he suggested sarcastically.

"Hmm...I'm not so sure," God muttered, shuffling his cards around. "Is it any good?"

We both gaped at him open mouthed.

"I was talking to him," Nick responded.

"Oh. Of course," God answered quickly. "I knew that!"

"So, you *have* read the bible then?" Nick asked. Unlike me he was not willing to let this one pass by so easily. We all have our issues, I suppose.

"Some of it..." God replied, squirming just a little. "But

generally I prefer the writings of the Shan-Tao and the Mayan people. Oh...here's a thought! Did you know that the Mayan's predicted that the end of the world would occur on December twenty first two thousand and twelve? That would have solved a lot of our problems wouldn't it? We could have started all over again. Those ancient civilisations were way ahead of their time in some respects."

Was he joking, I wondered? It was hard to tell.

He set down the card with Valentina's face on it and I knew at that moment that she was either dead or else extremely close to it. It was time for me to go - and besides I really didn't want to hear any more. I found the reality of heaven far too depressing.

"I'd better go," I said, excusing myself.

"Sure," God replied with an absent minded nod. "You're doing a great job. With a little more focus you will achieve great things. Be sure to stop by again on Thursday night – Gabriel here will be doing a solo performance of The Proclaimers greatest hits."

"Ok...thanks," I muttered.

Could this be any more surreal?

My mind was racing as I hurried back down the stairway, holding onto the thrumming handrail as it vibrated with strange hidden forces. There must be a way to help Valentina and do my job at the same time, I thought frantically. I just hoped she wasn't dead already else there was no chance. I quickly ran through the rules that governed my job, wondering if there was anyway round them.

At no time must I use my powers to resurrect a victim who has passed beyond the second realm.

At no time must I manifest myself physically to intervene

in cases that involve loss of life or the use of violent force.

Until all aspects of training are completed, deadly force must only be used against a subject when specifically sanctioned by the Supreme Being himself.

Absolute control over a subject's thought process via possession is strictly prohibited. But the power of suggestion maybe used via manipulation of emotions, hormones, sleeping patterns and dreams.

That last one gives me pause for thought. It allowed for a certain amount of improvisation on my part. The semblance of a plan started to form in my mind and by the time I stepped back into Casey's reality I knew exactly what way I was going to play this.

But the scene that greeted me when I arrived back brought me up short. Inevitably it was a sad and distressing one. I had only been gone a short time but it looked as though a rampaging beast has been let loose in the room, which is quite an apt analogy as he was exactly that.

The room has been utterly ransacked. Drawers lay open everywhere and tables sat overturned or else broken. In the centre of the floor, Valentina's half naked body lay bleeding and torn with a blade still embedded in her chest. As Casey rolled off her she took one last shuddering breath. An unexpected rage welled up inside me giving me the confidence to make my move.

It's down to me to stop this!

I followed that last tremulous inhalation as it flowed downwards into her lungs, making my way swiftly into her blood stream. I was searching and seeking - looking for a particular place. A very important one.

Two seconds was all it took to find what I was looking for -

the twin adrenal glands sitting atop Valentina's kidneys. Once again I felt sick with worry.

God, this job was so stressful!

I'd never done this before and I had no idea what the consequences would be. Nevertheless I felt determined to do it. I'd committed myself now. There was no going back.

Carefully I focused a limited amount of my energies outwards, unleashing an electrical charge in the direction of those two odd little triangular glands. Adrenaline immediately flooded Valentina's system prompting her to take another ragged breath. It was sort of like using a defibrillator, only better.

Her lungs filled with air as I forced platelets and other clotting agents to the sites of her many injuries. I was hoping it would be enough to save her but it would be touch and go whether or not I succeeded. Although all this kept me intensely occupied I could still hear the emergency services approaching in the distance prompting Casey to hastily pull up his trousers. He was ready for off. Getting caught was not on his current list of aspirations.

There was no way I could let him get away with this again. Not this time. I'd spent the last week or so poring over his file and what I had seen had disgusted me.

I took control of Valentina's mind and body and reached out for him with her bloodied hand.

"Get off bitch!" he started to say. But he never got any further than the word off. Valentina's hand suddenly became a conduit for my considerable powers and I gladly used it to deliver a paralyzing bolt of energy into his spinal cord.

With just one zap his lips wilted midsentence and he slumped to the floor like a piece of over-cooked spaghetti. For all intents and purposes he appeared dead. But I could tell he was fully conscious. I could almost hear his panicked chaotic thoughts - the frantic swearing and whimpering of someone who had found himself locked in. He was probably kicking the walls of his mental prison cell doing his level best to get out. I felt no sympathy.

The connection was still in place between the three of us so I transferred about sixty per cent of his life force into Valentina. The effect was noticeable to me immediately.

Her swelling, bruising and bleeding began to subside and the healing process sped up dramatically. I smile inwardly at my apparent success. Finally I was getting somewhere!

The paramedics and police burst in just as she was returning to consciousness. They buzzed around talking rapidly into their radios, taking her blood pressure, pulse and temperature. One of them held her hand and talked kindly to her whilst another one set up an IV.

Upon seeing that she was in good hands now I relaxed a little. But there was just one last thing I had to do before I left. My prime objective had not yet been fulfilled.

Steeling myself I entered the now drastically subdued mind of Casey Davenport who was still lying paralyzed on the acacia wood floor. One lone paramedic was working on him, methodically and thoroughly. No one wanted to be accused of not doing their job properly.

"Hello Casey," I said in a hollow grating whisper.

"Who's that?" he stammered. Mentally he backed away unsure of what had just happened.

The sound of flapping wings echoed within the darkest caverns of his brain as I set about increasing the Norepinephrine levels and decreasing his Serotonin - both of which would fuel his growing anxiety. After all, those were the hormones responsible for panic attacks. God's assistant He'vernon had taught me well. She was smart as well as beautiful.

"What is this shit?" he moaned.

As though I was leaning forward right next to his left ear I whispered loudly, "It's Karma, Casey. Ya know? What goes around, comes around?"

"I'm not afraid of you!" he bawled, his voice reverberating inside his own head. "You're just a bad fucking trip. That's all."

"No Casey," I told him, closing off his windpipe. "I'm very real. Else how could I have just cut off your air supply?"

He choked and spluttered. Out in the real world he suddenly turned hypoxic. The paramedics converged upon him en mass, unsure of what had gone wrong. I ignored them and carried on with my mission.

"You're right about one thing," I continued menacingly. "I am going away. Just for a little while…You see I have an important meeting with a guy at two o'clock. Someone you may have heard of actually. He goes by several names; the Devil, Satan, Beelzebub etc etc But between you and me we're pretty tight, so he lets me call him Nick. Anyways, it would seem he needs a few more permanent residents for Hell – which is a kind of specialist resort he runs – apparently he was wondering if I might know of anyone…"

Suddenly I released his windpipe and I heard him gasping wildly for air – forcing it into his lungs like it was going out of fashion.

"Don't send me to Hell," he rasped. "I'll do anything."

"Hell?" I laughed mercilessly.

Ahhh…it was so much fun winding this scumbag up!

"Are you serious? Hell is far too good for you, you filthy rotten piece of dog phlegm. You my friend are staying right here, for a very, very long time."

"NOooooo……" he yelled.

At that point I just smiled and left him to it before making my way back to the fifth dimension.

Chapter Three

The Victory

SOMEONE WAS SLAPPING my back as I stepped into heaven. What on earth was going on?

"Hey...way to go Karma!" said a seraphim with shimmering golden wings. "God told us what went down with Casey."

He was slapping me on the back like I'd just scored a touchdown for the Cardinals or something. Several other angels hovered nearby also murmuring their approval.

"What do you mean?" I asked feeling a little confused.

In the three weeks that I'd been in training for the position, this was the first anybody had acknowledged anything I'd done besides He'vernon. It was as if I'd been invisible and I hated to admit it but it had made me feel pretty lonely.

"Why, saving Valentina, of course!" he grinned. "Can't wait to see what you do with that scumbag Davenport. He should have been stopped long ago."

"My thoughts exactly," I responded darkly.

A flock of cherubs suddenly flew beneath me and carried me away on their tiny backs.

"Well done Karma," one of them said patting me on the leg. "The boss wants to see you now."

With that they let me go and I fell through the pastel coloured clouds like a stone. I seemed to fall forever – arms flailing through the cottony layers. Eventually I stopped as though held in a tractor beam like the one they used in that old fashioned space travel series on TV.

For a while no one said anything. I was just held suspended in mid-air. My patience was certainly taking a battering today. Understandably I began to wonder what was going on. Was some impish little cherub playing a practical joke or was there something more sinister at work?

"Put me down!" I ordered. "I've got work to do."

Very carefully someone lowered me to the ground and out from the ether stepped God himself.

I nodded my head in deference to his position.

"Almighty," I said tersely. I was still feeling pretty revved up from what I had witness down below. His attitude soon put the damper on that.

"Well Karma!" he boomed. "I see you've been busy."

"Yes, I have."

"What on earth were you thinking boy?" he rumbled.

This was a far cry from the easy going deity I'd witnessed playing cards earlier. He seemed pretty ticked off. Or maybe that had just been his Saturday night persona…

"I'm not sure what you're referring to," I quailed, although I had a sneaking feeling I knew.

"I'm referring to the fact that you've practically imprisoned a subject instead of administering a long overdue dose of good old fashioned karma. You were supposed to kill him. Did I not make that clear enough?" he asked, fixing me with a penetrating stare. "Not to mention that you altered Valentina's fate."

It was no good squirming. I had to stand by the choices I'd made.

"Well, yes I did alter her fate," I admitted. "But there's nothing in the four laws of Karma to say I couldn't, as long as I didn't materialise into human form to do it. As for Casey Davenport, I like to consider him as being in a state of transition. He will get his just desserts, but *my* way and in a way that will make a lasting impression."

I said this last part with apparent conviction but inside I was cringing at my outspoken little speech. After all, he *was* The Almighty.

"So I take it you *do* have plans for him then? You're not just going to leave him that way?"

"I haven't quite decided what to do with him yet, but rest assured I'll do my job and without breaking the four laws," I promised.

God fell silent and looked out into the distance towards the lake of rainbows.

"To be frank with you, I feel somewhat apprehensive," he said turning round slowly. "It seems to me that you're doing your best to push the boundaries, to bend the rules as much as possible without actually breaking them. Looking for loop holes even and I have no idea why. If I tolerate it, what kind of message do you think I'm sending out to the others? Things have been done this way for millennia and for good reason. Who are you to come along and change a tried and tested system of doing things?"

"Look," I said, sounding a lot calmer than I actually felt. "I have a funny feeling about this guy. For some reason, once it actually came down to it, I just couldn't see my way clear to bumping him off immediately. At least not without giving him a chance to see where he went wrong. The way I see it, after everything he's done I would be letting him off the hook far too easily."

God looked at me in the oddest way, as though he was suffering from indigestion or something.

"What you mean is you really want to make this guy suffer," he said hopefully.

"Not exactly. Look, I know it sounds crazy," I continued, trying my best to explain. "If ever there was a clear open and shut Karma case it's him. But I was wondering…have any of the other previous Karma's tried to re-educate a subject prior to final sentencing? You know, make them see the error of their ways and pay penance etc…"

I had to ask him, because I had no personal memories beyond three weeks ago. The moment I had started my training to take on the role of Karma all memories linking me to my past were wiped in order for me to be able to make impartial decisions. Basically I had no idea who I was, or how long I'd been in heaven. I was a blank canvas. However God had assured me that this was the way it had always been done.

"No. I don't believe they have," said God frowning. "All the other Karmas were quite content with dropping their subjects down lift shafts from twenty stories up or smiting them with some horrendous flesh eating disease. It would be much easier for everyone if you just followed suit instead of trying to be some kind of maverick."

"Yes, but in the grand scheme of things, does it really matter how I do things as long as I get the job done? Let me just try doing it my way, just this once. See how it turns out. What do you say?" I begged.

I knew I was being way too familiar.

He looked at me long and hard, then pointed a faintly glowing finger towards me. The urge to take a step backwards was overwhelming. But I resisted.

"Alright," he said magnanimously. "Have it your way. I'll let you have free reign on this one. But the rules still stand. Remember that."

That last statement irked me, as the rules were just about all I had in my head as far as memories went, but I decided to say nothing about that. That was a subject for another day; after I'd proved myself.

As though he had read my mind he began to extolling the virtues of doing things by the book and how it was all about taking into consideration the bigger picture – that we were all like cogs in a well-oiled machine. I just nodded dumbly in all the right places, but I'd already made up my mind that no matter what, Casey Davenport was going to be made an example of *and* if at all possible he was going to learn where he went wrong before he left the mortal plane of existence.

That was *my* bigger picture.

Chapter Four

The Dark

AS THE BUS juddered along Hector Street, Valentina looked down at her fading scars. The sun shone brightly through the dusty window warming her petite brown hands as she held them wonderingly up to the light.

Just over a week ago, they'd been a complete mess. Cut to the bone and the nerves severed, it had taken the surgeons over three hours just to fix her hands. She had scars in other places, too. Those would take longer to heal.

Taken as a whole though, she'd made a remarkable recovery, surprising everyone with her resilience, especially her aged mother who had always been one for thinking the worst. The pleasure she gained initially from her daughter's recovery was now overshadowed by the journey she was taking.

Her mother had been dumbfounded when Valentina expressed her desire to visit Casey. She did her best to talk her out of it. It just wasn't necessary to put herself through that she insisted. She'd been through enough without having to see that disgusting monster again. There were others whose duty it was to pray by his bedside, such as his family and the local pastor, she told her.

But Valentina would not hear of it. It was as if she was being driven by some inner force. Suffice to say that force was me.

When the bus drew up outside Rivendell County Hospital, Valentina stood stiffly to join the queue of people slowly disembarking. Left to her own devices, she would have had no idea which hospital he was in or which ward, but that information was easily planted with the false memory of a telephone conversation she'd had with her liaison officer.

Without hesitation she went in through the main entrance and followed the signs for ward nine west. As she made her way through the maze of corridors I decided to pay Casey a quick visit to prepare him for Valentina's arrival.

I hovered over him for a few brief seconds, looking down at his expressionless face. His eyes were open, yet fixed upon nothing. The only senses I'd left functioning were his hearing and sense of touch. I wanted him to be truly cut off – locked in completely, a prisoner within his own body so that he could reflect upon the course of his life. Looking at him still repulsed me but seeing him so vulnerable, so completely at my mercy caused me to feel something I didn't want to feel. I felt a twinge of pity. Angry with myself I brushed it aside. This man did not deserve anyone's pity. He was scum.

It had been eight days since I'd had any contact with him. The last time had been on the night of the attack. His current condition or state of mind was unknown to me. I had no idea what I might find once inside. Reluctantly I pushed inside his mind only to be greeted by silence.

"Casey!" I called out.

My voice echoed across the featureless wasteland. It was grey and barren - the colour of ash. Perhaps God had been right after all. Maybe I'd made an error in judgement and he'd gone quietly mad inside the confines of his own brain. But would that be such a bad thing, I wondered? Maybe that could be his Karma. But what would that achieve? He'd never learn anything if he went raving mad.

"Casey!" I shouted once more.

I stopped for a moment when I heard a sound coming from a dark recess tucked away in the back of his mind. I drifted over and took a look inside.

It was a sinister looking place oozing negative energies and decay.

There was that sound again. A faint humming that rose and fell like a haunting lullaby.

I stood at the entrance not wanting to go in - a feeling vaguely akin to dread washing over me. For some reason this place had an unnerving effect upon me. This was ridiculous, I told myself. Nothing could hurt me here.

In spite of my best efforts to convince myself otherwise, my feet stayed rooted to the spot as though held in shackles. Who knew what horrors lurked there or how it might affect me to witness them? I wanted to back away – to leave and never come back. But I still had a job to do. I began to think I should have listened to God and just killed him off when I'd had the chance. That would have kept things simple. That was one of my flaws – over analysing things. God did not want a Karma that mulled over every little detail. He wanted someone who followed orders. He had wanted

Casey dispatched – as simple as that. Perhaps if I was lucky my mistake could still be rectified.

Suddenly a bright orange light appeared as though someone had lit a match. The strange humming increased as the orangey light outlined the silhouette of Casey's back. He was rocking back and forth as he watched a scene playing out within his subconscious. Spellbound I watched as it unfolded before us almost like a movie or the script within a novel...

A small child lay in its mother's arms, inconsolable with pain. Her little legs drawn high up to her chest as she howled through tiny quivering lips.

"Celine!" a voice shouted.

A man had just walked in through the front door of their house. He sounded very angry.

"Here. Take Josephine," whispered the child's mother. She handed the baby over to her young son standing at her elbow.

"Mama, no!" he whispered. "Don't go."

Desperation and fear were etched deeply into his features. His little chocolate button eyes were wide and bright. Anxiety had made them so. She assumed he did not understand what she had to do. But he was a smart boy and worldly wise. He knew alright and it pained him.

"Be brave little man," she said stroking his face. "Some things just have to be done, whether we like them or not."

For a moment she appeared beautiful and sensitive, like the mother he used to know – before the spectre of his father's addiction had stolen her from them.

But the present situation necessitated survival mode if her children were to continue breathing for any length of time. Her mask of detachment slipped firmly back into place again as she hastily changed into a neon pink mini skirt and a metallic silver boob tube.

"Celine! Where are you, you stupid bitch?" growled the man.

The boy could hear him taking the stairs two at a time as was his habit when he wished to vent his spleen.

"I'm here!" she said, quickly stepping through the bedroom door. She shut it behind her carefully.

The baby set up howling again.

"Shhh," said the boy, rocking her. "Casey's here."

"What the fuck is wrong with that child?" the man growled, standing outside the door.

"She's ill Cal, that's all," said their mother.

"I hope you ain't been spendin' more money on her. There's nothing wrong with her that a good hiding wouldn't cure," he muttered, running his fingers over the woman's cleavage.

She flinched away from his touch, her feeling for him long since wasted. He retaliated by cuffing her hard. But there was no response in her heart.

She wiped away a trickle of blood where her teeth had sunk into her fulsome lips under the impact.

"She's the reason we're strugglin' to make ends meet. All those stupid fucking tests!" he spluttered viciously. "And the doctors still don't know nothing.'"

"We're making ends meet just fine Cal!" she shot back. "It's your habit that's the problem! All the crack in Kansas wouldn't slake your appetite. It ain't poor little Josephine's fault she's sick!"

The boy gasped in the darkness of the room, shocked at his mother's grit. Even baby Josephine had quieted. He waited helplessly for the blows to begin, but instead he heard a violent choking.

Cold settled upon his heart. This was it. Cal was going to kill his Mom. He was strangling her. The moon shone through the window, holding him captive as time stood still. His heart darkened and froze simultaneously within the cage of his raw, aching chest.
He knew he should do something, but he had no idea what. Blind panic and age were his enemies. All he could do was sit on the floor and rock his sister. After a few seconds he heard his mother trying to say something. He held his breath, paying close attention, imagining it was the last thing he would ever hear her say.

"Don't!" she rasped. As the words broke free from her throat she gasped.

With that one word, Cal seemed to realise what he was doing and released his hold on her slender neck. Like a child waiting to hear a fairy tale Casey waited for the word sorry. It never came. Well he would be one day, he vowed. He'd make sure of that.

"Yeah well, none of the punters will want to screw you if I mess you up too much," his father said, as though he had to justify not murdering the mother of his children. He stood back and ran his fingers through his wiry hair.

She tried to stand up again, but didn't quite make it. Instead she sat on the floor breathing hard - wincing as she tried to move her neck. Josephine set up wailing again in response to the pain wracking her jaundiced body.

Cal scowled at the closed door.

"You touch those kids while I'm gone and I'll never turn tricks for you or your miserable drug habit again!" whispered Celine hoarsely.

Love for her children gave her strength. She stood up and forced herself to leave the house – damping down the terror she felt at leaving her children alone with the maniac that was her husband. The man stood in the hallway and watched her leave, totally at peace in the knowledge that she was headed for the red light district.

As an afterthought he tried to summon up a modicum of rage at the thought of her selling herself to other men. But they needed the money. Correction. He needed the money.

In his opinion, the drugs made him a better man. They made him happy. When he was happy everyone was happy. It was only recently that things had changed.

The moment that baby had arrived on the scene, money had been scarce. Those tests were expensive. And pointless.

Pointless because in his drug warped view point she wasn't really a living breathing human being anyway. She was like some sort of pet. An annoyance. Something to be got rid of if he so wished.

As he lay on the couch listening to her screeching, coping with the dreaded aches and pains of drug withdrawal as best he could, he decided that he did wish it. Josephine had to go. She was too ill. It was time to put her down - for good.

As Casey heard him taking the stairs again, two at a time, something in the child's mind snapped. His mother wasn't there to protect them this time.

Death was coming. He could feel it.

Josephine was still screaming blue murder and there was nothing he could do. He looked around the room in desperation, frantically searching for a solution. His eyes homed in on his mother's closet. Operating purely on instinct he scrambled inside and shut the door. On the shelf above him he felt about and found a pillow. Without even a pause he grabbed it and held it firmly over the child's face pressing down as he rocked her gently. All he could think about was making her stop. If she would only be quiet they would both be safe.

Sick as she was, she barely struggled and when her legs stopped kicking his heart took on another layer of stone. It crossed his mind that perhaps she was grateful. A sick little smile played across his lips.

The bedroom door opened and his breath hitched. He couldn't help it. The fear Cal inspired was nauseating. All he could feel was an unearthly dread. The type that most people only experience in nightmares or at death.

"Bout fucking time!" Cal muttered glancing about the room. He seemed to think that Josephine had finally gone to sleep. Once he was sure his father had gone back downstairs Casey lifted the pillow and gazed down at his little sister.

Her eyes were closed. She looked peaceful – with her nose slightly upturned from the pressure of the pillow.

Although he was only seven, somewhere in his head he knew what he had done. It didn't matter to him that there were extenuating circumstances. His soul was a fractured mirror now and there would never be any going back.

He sat there and cradled her body for two hours, feeling the warmth slowly draining away from her. For three months she'd been alive and all she'd ever experienced was pain. That thought made him angry - blinding him. Making him crazy. Someone was going to pay.

He stood up slowly, feeling old beyond his years and placed Josephine's body gently on the counterpane. He stared at her for a time long. Nothing seemed real anymore. Suffering had finally discovered his limits. He opened the bedside draw where he found a cigarette lighter. Gingerly he crept downstairs.

There on the couch Cal lay fast asleep blissfully unaware of what had just happened. Although he was ugly as sin and as big as a bear Casey no longer felt afraid. He narrowed his eyes in anger unwilling to forgive any longer. It was the work of a moment to set fire to the drapes, tablecloth and unused nappies piled up in one corner of the room. He felt no regret as he watched it burn. No sadness. Nothing. Only hate.

By the time the fire services arrived, the blaze had engulfed the entire living room and everything in it – including Cal. On the front porch, they found Casey – a morsel of broken humanity with burning debris falling round his shoulders as he idly flicked the cigarette lighter.

I stood watching the scene shrouded in darkness as they hustled the young boy away. The scene faded to nothing but Casey still sat with his back to me flicking an imaginary cigarette lighter open and closed. I say imaginary, because everything was imaginary in this plain of existence.

"Was that real?" I asked him in a neutral voice.

He made no reply.

I decided the situation warranted my visible presence rather than a disembodied voice, so I walked over and crouched down beside him.

"Casey, was that real?" I repeated, laying a heavy hand on his shoulder.

"Yes, IT WAS FUCKING REAL!" he barked, his eyes literally blazing mere inches from mine. His anger was palpable. Out in the real world, back in the hospital, the door to his room opened and in walked Valentina. Casey heard the chair creak as she sat down next to his bed.

"Who's that?" he said, forcing his anger to take a back seat. It would seem he was not used to having visitors. Small wonder considering the circles he mixed in.

"It's Valentina," I told him, watching for his reaction.

"Who's Valentina? I don't know anyone called Valentina."

"The woman you raped," I said simply.

"Yeah right," he chuckled.

"No. I'm serious. She's sitting right next to you."

He stopped smiling and threw down the lighter.

"What's she here for?" he snapped. "Revenge?"

"You'd better hope not, because you're completely at her mercy lying here."

"Well, is she or not?" he said, looking nervous.

"Well, just ask yourself, what would you do in her situation? Then you'll have your answer," I said with a sadistic smile.

"You've got to let me out of here," he said, looking desperate. "You can't just let her kill me."

"Why not?" I said, shrugging my shoulders. "No one would care. I'd be doing the world a favour."

"Because it ain't right. I can't even move," he protested.

"Since when did you care about what's right and wrong?" I demanded. "Did you care about such things when you shot Antony Williams in the face and left him lying in a pool of blood for his wife and kids to find? Or when you beat that Chinese hooker within an inch of her life because she owed you fifty dollars and couldn't pay? I could go on. It's a pretty big list."

"What can I say?" he admitted, throwing his hands up. "From my perspective, life's always been cheap. And that hooker deserved it. She'd no intention of paying up."

Suddenly, he cocked his head to one side as though listening for something.

"What's that sound?" he asked. There was a strange whispering coming from somewhere. "What's she saying?"

"It's Valentina. She's praying," I replied.

"Praying?" he said in disbelief. "What kind of nut job is she? Doesn't she know there's no one up there?"

"She's praying for your soul," I answered solemnly. "So you'd better hope she's damn good at it!"

With that I left him to it and went upstairs to speak with God again.

No one congratulated me upon my arrival this time. I caught one or two eyeing me with a certain amount of curiosity but apart from that I was ignored.

"How come you never informed me about Casey's troubled childhood?" I said to God once, inside his plush office. It was truly immense. In fact I couldn't see the other side.

"Because that should have absolutely no impact on your decision. Your path is a simple one, devise a method of Karma commensurate with his crimes and enact it. How he got to this point is none of your business," he said signing a raft of papers with a flourish. "You were not supposed to 'see' his distant past. I've got to hand it to you Karma, your unconventional methodology has certainly complicated things."

Hundreds of wall mounted large screen TVs covered the walls of his office. All of them showed scenes from planet earth. As far as I could see they were divided into two sections – an engraved marble plaque above each. One read Humdrum, the other one, Not So Humdrum.

I took a quick glance at what was going on in the Humdrum section: a gathering of world leaders to discuss climate change, a tsunami heading for a group of islands in the Pacific, a man strapping explosives to himself in the Middle East. In some of them I had no idea what was going on.

In the Not So Humdrum section I could see worshippers gathering at Mecca, a colourful Hindu festival taking place, a pilgrim climbing a mountain on his knees and the final results of XFactor.

God looked at me and smiled.

"Don't you just love this time of year?" he said happily.

I smiled tightly and attempted to pick up our previous discussion where it had left off.

"Yes, but getting back to the subject of Casey, if there is a reason for his behaviour surely I need to take that into consideration?" I persisted.

"No, you don't. All you need to know is that he had a choice. He didn't have to become what he is. Lots of people go through similar things - that's the way life is down there. Not all of them end up as vicious murderers," God pointed out.

61

"Well, perhaps he could change given the chance," I told him.

"It is not your job to change him!" thundered God. "It is your job to teach humans that sometimes bad deeds catch up with them and bite them on the ass!"

I nodded vigorously in agreement and stared down at my toes. Boy had I made him mad! The air had become charged with static electricity due to his outburst. As I stood before him I could feel every hair on my body standing on end. I could see that I'd rumpled his feathers again so I decided to change the subject a little before he blew me to atoms.

"I do have one more question before I go…"

"Yes," he said, raising an eyebrow expectantly.

"The part of Casey's mind that he'd retreated to during that flash back of his childhood, why did it give me the creeps? Is that normal?" I asked cautiously.

God's countenance now resumed that supremely patient expression he generally wore.

"Of course it's normal. Anyone worthy of being in heaven would find such a place deeply unnerving. It was not a situation you were supposed to face. But what is done, is done. Hopefully you now realise the importance of expediency in this case. It is time this 'matter' was resolved," he said firmly.

The problem was I really couldn't decide. If I was honest I knew I wanted to make Casey suffer a bit. There was no question about that, but for some reason I didn't think I couldn't bring myself to kill him and I knew that's what everyone was expecting.

A few weeks later, I checked in on Valentina as once again she was at the hospital visiting Casey and was surprised to find a certain situation developing - one that I had not been foreseen.

Valentina was pregnant.

I assumed that she would just arrange for an abortion when she found out but that was not the case. The young woman had deep seated religious beliefs and would not even consider it regardless of what anyone else advised. Frustratingly, this gave me even more to consider and complicated the case even further.

Until one day it struck me that Casey's reaction to the news might be the decider as to what degree of karma I should mete out. Choosing when to tell him was the hard part. Even though I still had regular conversations with Casey I decided to keep this new information from him until closer to the time. His anger didn't seem quite so pronounced these days and sometimes I even suspected that he was glad to see me.

He even asked me details about myself on one occasion, so I fed him some mocked up cover story about my previous life on earth.

I have to say that seemed to eat away at me for a while, not having anything real to tell him. I was beginning to feel very dissatisfied that I had very little substance as an individual. I knew nothing about myself on any level – all my experiences were recent ones and all my preferences were new. But that was what being Karma required.

Week after week, month after month God kept dragging me into his office and raking me over the coals for not bringing the case to a swift conclusion. Time after time I reassured him that I was following a distinct path that I'd set out and that Casey would finally taste Karma in the truest sense. It seemed as though we were locked in a perpetual cycle of conflict, but eventually that cycle was broken when one day Valentina failed to appear at Casey's bedside.

To the outsider, this had no effect on him whatsoever. For all intents and purposes he was just a cabbage, with nothing going on upstairs. But inside, I knew that Casey Davenport was pacing up and down worrying about whether or not his only contact with the outside world was ever coming back.

I decided to leave him for a bit and let him stew. For nine days Casey had no contact whatsoever barring the nurses who came in briefly to change the sheets and wash him etc. None of them spoke to him.

It was like he was already dead.

By the end of the ninth day he was wishing he *was* dead and had begun to wither away mentally. I decided the time had come to pay him another visit.

"Well, well, well," I said, when I found him down on his knees praying.

Hastily he stood up and turned to face me.

"Where have you been?" he exclaimed, dragging his fingers down his face. "I've been going crazy in here! Where's Valentina? Why hasn't she been?"

"She's in hospital," I told him. "Complications from the birth."

"Birth? What birth?" he said looking bewildered.

"The birth of your daughter," I replied.

His mouth hung open but no words came out. He shook his head and started pacing around in circles again.

"Shit!" he exclaimed. "Shit, shit, shit."

I left him alone to digest this latest piece of information.

When I returned a few days later he had changed completely. He bounded up to me the moment I appeared.

"I want to see her," he said gruffly.

"See who?"

"My daughter."

"I'm afraid you can't."

"Yeah, but you've got special powers and shit. You can make it happen," he said hopefully. "I can change if you give me the chance."

This was exactly what I'd been hoping for – that he would realise that he had the capability to change. Problem was I didn't have the power to give him that opportunity. All I could do was impose Karma. So basically I'd been wasting my time I thought glumly. The time for procrastination had reached its end. Like someone who couldn't yet swim, I was faced with the task of dipping my toes into the water…It was time to render judgement on this most dissolute of souls.

"Even if I could do it, I wouldn't," I lied. "It's time justice was served – others must see what befalls people like you and learn to fear treading the same path that bought you here. In the eyes of many your sentence may seem to be a lenient one, as the crimes you have committed unquestionably deserve the death penalty. But after already living this way for nine months you may not agree. Being locked in is no picnic. Casey Davenport, I hereby exact the following penalty of Karma: You will never have full control over this body again. You will be locked in for the remainder of your earthly days, unable to see or speak."

"Please! Give me a chance!" he begged, dropping to his knees again. "I want to see her! I have rights!"

His petitions were fruitless. The sentence was sealed with a resounding hammer strike from above.

It was harder than I thought leaving him like that but I really believed I'd made the best possible choice. A straight forward death was too good for him. I wanted him to think about what he had done for a really long time. And as long as he was still alive there was always a chance that he could surprise us all and do something good, even if it was only changing his way of thinking. Now it was time to return to heaven for my debriefing, which is kind of an odd concept, really. What possible information could I have that God wouldn't already know?

I puzzled over this as I climbed the eternal stairway to heaven. By the time I reached the top I knew something was up. God didn't need to be debriefed. There had to be another reason he wished to see me. I had no clue what that might be, but if he was reluctant to be upfront about it chances were it was not going to be good.

I'd had enough of constantly provoking his displeasure. And what's more, I wanted to know who I really was. I wanted to be a person again, not just a title.

"I quit," I told him the moment I walked into his office.

"What?" he said, looking mightily confused.

"I said I quit."

"But why? You're just getting the hang of it," he replied making an obvious effort to placate me. "It took a while, but you got there in the end."

"I've had enough of constantly going head to head with you. We just don't see eye to eye," I told him. "From what you said, all the other Karma's fitted neatly into this role. I don't. I don't belong here and I'm not the only one who thinks so. All this time I've spent and I haven't even completed the training yet!"

Suddenly I felt as if everything in the universe had decided to focus on me. Everything slowed down and his next words were expelled from his mouth like the stirrings of a summer zephyr.

"Ok, I accept your resignation. I suppose you still want to know who you are?" he said, changing the subject blithely. I could sense an audience, even though I could see none.

I nodded dumbly.

"Very well. This is the true you," he said, casually holding up a splendid full length mirror. It had magically became manifest in a blinding flash of light.

The reflection of Cal Davenport stared back at me. We both took a step back – both as stunned as each other. I frowned. So did he. Then the horrible truth dawned on me – dawned on 'us.' We were one and the same. Our movements synchronised. Our expressions matched in every detail.

That was me. I was the baby killer. The man who'd pimped out his own wife for drugs and exposed his son to the kind of horrors that no child should ever see. I was the man from the flashback.

It was too much to take in. I couldn't believe it. My mind, my soul sought to find grounds to reject it.

"That's not me," I said, still in denial. "It doesn't make sense."

"It makes perfect sense," said God rolling his eyes. "Yet again this is a truth that you were never supposed to see but as always you insisted on knowing everything."

I turned away in despair.

"Is that why I felt the way I did when I saw the flash back of Casey's childhood?"

He nodded.

"Memories are easy to erase. But emotional imprints connected to certain events are not."

"Oh my God!" I shouted, holding my head in my hands. "You've just let me judge my own son! My own son no less! I've sentenced him to a living hell!"

"So what?" God shrugged. "You know he deserves it."

"Does he? DOES HE? What about me? What do I deserve then?" I cried.

"You got what you deserved. You've been burning in hell for the last twenty three years. Then you got a lucky break when a double agent position came up. Both Nick and I thought the position would suit. Your predecessor agreed with us," he explained. "Granted your personal memories had to be erased but we both thought your inherent dominance and natural vindictiveness made you well suited to the job. Within a few weeks of training you were polishing up quite well, although it was quite ironic that your first case was your own son. A sort of naturally occurring karma."

He seemed to find this quite amusing.

"Send me back!" I ordered him angrily. "I want to die."

"Don't be ridiculous," he sneered, taking out a nail file and filing his nails. "You already are dead. The only place left to you now is Hell."

"Whatever," I muttered, no longer caring.

"Suit yourself," he shrugged, lifting a tiny pentagonal shaped remote control.

I gritted my teeth and braced myself for what lay ahead.

"One other thing though before you go," he said, setting the remote back down on his gargantuan desk.

"What?" I asked in a voice wrung dry of all hope.

"You need to assign a successor, someone who you feel will do the job well."

The answer was easy. Praise be! There was hope after all. "Casey."

"Casey?" he snorted. "It has to be someone who's dead already."

"Well, he's as good as - thanks to me," I replied. "No one will notice him gone. This is his chance to make good. He's the perfect man for the job."

The supreme being looked deep in thought. He appeared to be giving it serious consideration.

"Promise me one thing though?" I said.

"What?"

"Leave his memories where they are!" I said eyeing him boldly. "Else all you've got is a fucking automaton."

He scowled and lifted the remote control, zapping me straight back to Hell.

"Train him well!" I cried as I fell smiling into the unquenchable flames.

"We will," came the faint reply.

Chapter Five

Unknown Quantities

"I DON'T KNOW why you promised him that," said the Devil accusingly.

He was standing with his back to the pearly gates chatting with God over what had just transpired.

"I think you're forgetting who I am," God replied, straightening his unbelievably pristine white collar. "I can promise whatever the hell I want."

"Take it easy," said the Devil raising his hands. "I'm just saying that it's going to be a tough one to deliver. If you can't erase his memories you're going to have to work with what you've got. And Casey isn't exactly Mother Teresa if you know what I'm saying. For all we know he may not even want the job."

"He will, given the right motivation," said God with a knowing smiling.

The Devil chuckled and shook his head.

"And I thought I was the wily one," he laughed.

He seemed to consider pressing him for more information,

but then thought better of it.

"You know who we should use on this job?" he said brightly. "That guy Tupac. I could spare him for a little while. Those two have a lot in common. He would listen to him."

"I don't think so," replied God. "We want him to become Karma, not a member of The Black Panther Party. No. We need an unknown to persuade him. Someone from my side of town with no prior connections."

"That sounds pretty one sided. I'm not sure I can agree to that. If you want my co-operation you going to have to oil the gears a bit," said the Devil.

"Oil the gears? What are we talking about here? You expect me to give you serious input after that stunt you pulled with the Catholic Church – making sure all the latent paedophiles were ordained as priests? I know temptation is one of your main fields of interests Nick – but that was just going too far."

"Pah! You're only annoyed because it turned people away from you."

"So I didn't like the bad press. What of it?"

"I knew it!" shouted Nick, slapping his knee in triumph.

"Look, let's just put that to one side for a moment shall we?" God said, forcing a smile. "There are bigger issues at stake here. Listen! How does this sound? You rustle us up a victim worthy of some serious Karma, and then we can use it as a test case for Casey. It has to be something that holds some significance for him. Something personal."

"You know what to do," he said patting the Devil's shoulder. "I'll sort the rest. Deal?"

"Ok. Deal," agreed Satan, licking his lips with a scarlet

tongue. Steam rose up from the slit of his mouth and his eyes narrowed in hunger. He fell to his knees as ten curved claws ripped through his shiny black shoes, destroying them beyond all repair. Seconds later a set of sickly yellowed talons erupted from his manicured nails and he roared with the force of ten thousand lions.

"Restrain yourself!" God chastised him in annoyance. "Or go back from whence you came."

"My pleasure," the Devil panted. The material of his black pure wool suit split and two powerful scarlet wings burst forth.
With a volley of flaps from his monstrous wingspan he was gone and God was left alone again on the Plain of Solitude to take full measure of the current situation.

Looking almost weary he removed his sandals and sat on the edge of a cloud bank, centring his thoughts – trying to find calm.

It had been a long time since he had come across a situation that troubled him the way this one did. For some reason God was having difficulty projecting his mind far enough into the future to foresee where all this was going. Things were heavily clouded with regard to Casey which was part of the reason why he had wanted him killed off. He didn't like encountering unknown quantities. In truth it wasn't supposed to happen at all and to make matters worse not only had Casey survived the Karma process but he'd been nominated for the position himself!

That would unsettle anyone he told himself especially when you took into account that Karma's actions tended to reflect upon him. He needed to have someone in the position he could rely on, someone who would consider the ramifications of his actions. Up until now Casey's life's work resembled the actions of a madman.

God doubted he was even capable of thinking of anyone besides himself.

If Casey was going to take on the position he would have to undergo some serious character transformation first. Somebody would have to train him. Finding someone suitable would be difficult. God had lots of people on his side with a manipulative streak a mile long. No doubt they would derive great satisfaction from making him toe the line. But he needed someone who had the power to mentor someone like him and effect a real change even then he'd probably need some sort of leverage against him just in case he went off the rails.

That would take a little more planning. For now though it was time to make his way to the Arena of Time where the heavenly hosts were waiting for his arrival.

Chapter Six

The Volunteer

THE ARENA WAS rumoured to be built from time itself – some portions frozen, some portions in a state of flux. To the untrained eye it looked as though it was made from some sort of opalescent amethyst, but in liquid form that had coagulated in numerous places forming shimmering crystalline columns that twisted upwards until they resembled massive unicorn horns. The seating consisted of rows and rows of shining palladium pews. Each one held twenty angels of varying types chattering animatedly with each other like old ladies on a bus.

The moment God appeared they all snapped to attention, except those at the very back that as of yet had failed to notice his arrival.

"Welcome!" God said in a voice that seemed to shake the very foundations.

"We are honoured," murmured the angels, bowing their heads till they almost touched their knees.

The meeting began with a breakdown of the latest events in

the universe, such as four suns goings super nova in the delta quadrant and the recent skirmishes between the Muslims and the Christians in Egypt. What everyone was really waiting for though was an explanation about what had gone on between Karma and Casey. Since Karma's disappearance the rumour mills had gone into over drive.

They were in for a disappointment as God chose to merely skim over it.

"So...in what I might add is a most unusual and highly unorthodox decision, Karma has appointed Casey as his successor," he said. Murmurs of dissent arose from those seated.

"This has left us with a challenging and somewhat perplexing problem. Although Casey Davenport has shown signs of changing his murderous mind set he is long way away from a complete rehabilitation. If he is to take on the role of Karma and discharge his duties in the proper manner he *must* be properly trained. So we need a volunteer," he announced, looking round expectantly.

For a moment everyone was so busy digesting this news that they all neglected to put up their hand. Gabriel who was seated next to God taking the minutes of the meeting, cleared his throat noisily.

At the sound of this poorly disguised prompt several hands flew up at once. God smiled indulgently.

"Thank you Sarah. I'm sure you will do an excellent job," he said, smoothing down his flowing ceremonial robes.

No one could see Sarah, as she was seated way over at the back of the arena. But her voice rang out indistinctly.

"Could you speak up please so that your comments can be

recorded in the minutes?" called Gabriel with a cheerful smile.

"I said, I never put my hand up. I didn't volunteer."

Gabriel's smile fell and his mouth formed a silent 'o' of surprise. He glanced over at God and shrugged his shoulders.

"Never mind my dear. I'm sure you will be perfect," God reassured her. "We can talk over the details in my office later."

He wasn't about to discuss anything here. Ironically the Arena of Time was neither the place nor the time for such a conversation.

Back in Rivendell County hospital, Casey Davenport lay still as a corpse in a perfectly crease free bed. The sheets had been changed that morning and since then he'd never moved a muscle. He never did.

That however didn't stop him from straining his ears in order to pick up every sound within the normal range of human hearing. That didn't require conscious movement. But it did require concentration and determination.

As his hearing was one of the few senses left open to him he focused on it fiercely in order to distract himself from one of the more troubling senses he had left – his sense of touch.

Touch had become a curse to him. Like his hearing it had become heightened until he was intensely focused on every sensation. After months and months of such heightened awareness, it had gotten to the stage where every nerve receptor on the surface of his body was extraordinarily sensitized. He longed to move just to relieve the pressure or to be able to scratch those insufferable itches that plagued him in the middle of the night. In the past these were simple things that he'd always taken for granted like most people, now they were luxuries that were quite literally way out of his reach.

His entire body was sore – especially where his skin contacted the bed and the bed clothes. The nurses were neglecting to change his diaper often enough, which left his private area red raw and brought his discomfort to an even more demeaning level.

If someone had told him a year ago that he'd end up in such a situation, he'd have laughed in their face. Yet here he was, rotting from the outside in and not a soul cared enough to spare him a second thought. If he could have put an end to his existence he would have. But he was powerless.

At night he lay awake for hours, struggling to shut down his troubled mind. His permanent state of physical and emotional discomfort meant that sleep was often just out of his grasp. It cruelly evaded him night after night until he came to the realisation that it was only when he gave up the pursuit that slumber overtook him.

He also learnt that to achieve any kind of emotional peace he had to control his thoughts. It was a lot easier to descend into the blissful numbness of sleep if he steered clear of the chaos surrounding his past. That meant visualising himself in a very different future and finding the singular ray of hope that would transport him there.

The difficult part was admitting that he needed hope at all. As a child, social workers and counsellors had tried to instil into him the value of hope and positive thinking but even then he had felt it was a sissy concept. As time went on he tended to avoid the path of introspective thinking by immersing himself in drugs, alcohol and his involvement in crime. Now that those avenues were closed to him he could do little else.

He now saw that his mind could be a powerful tool – an ally. But in order to achieve his ends he needed to subjugate it.
He thought about how he had been judged by Karma and why. Over the weeks and months he came to see that he had acted barbarically.

He'd inflicted pain and suffering on people who did not deserve it - people who had nothing to do with the savage anger and bitterness that had been eating away at him for all these years. The futility and ultimately the injustice of his actions stood out to him now as clearly as bloodstains upon snow.

If anything he'd fanned the flames of his anger – and look where it had gotten him. He'd burnt himself badly. That said, it still puzzled him that he'd been singled out from all the other myriads of people who could have been judged. Lots of other people he knew of had done worse things than him and what's more they had gotten away with it both in the eyes of the law and in the eyes of God – if there was such a thing.

Sometimes he wondered whether the whole thing had in fact been some kind of delusion he'd experienced from the drugs he'd taken on the night of the attack. But he had no way of knowing.

Eventually he started to cling to the notion that that's what had indeed happened. He preferred that truth because it allowed for the possibility that he may recover at some point. If his current situation was a result of supernatural intervention then there would be no escaping it. He would certainly die there, locked inside his own body like a fly trapped in amber. This was the thought that saved him from madness. He had finally found a grain of hope. The whole thing had been a delusion, he decided. Karma was not real after all.

What a relief!

The natural progression of such reasoning was that he thought more and more about escaping his bonds. There just had to be some way to get free – a key of some sort.

It had to be said his options were extremely limited. The one and only key he possessed was his mind and for now that didn't seem to fit in the lock. But that didn't mean it couldn't be adapted given time and a superhuman amount of determination.

He figured that if he worked hard enough he could improve his mental strength and resolve by stretching and pushing the limitations of his mind just as an athlete would train his muscles. Even in that he was limited.

The only way he could think of doing such a thing was by listening closely to everything that was happening around him on the hospital ward.

So he began straining his ears almost every waking moment and trying to process the information he garnered from doing so. This did precisely what he thought it would. It strengthened his mind. What he didn't foresee was that a valuable bi product of this was that it also served as a distraction from his situation.

One day he was lying listening to two nurses walking along the corridor outside his room. They were arguing over some new reality show that they'd both been watching.

Casey thought about the shows that he used to enjoy before his imprisonment. It had been a long time since he'd even seen anything with his own eyes let alone watched a TV show. Listening to such conversations was his only link with the outside world now that Valentina no longer visited him and he was always thirsty for news.

"I tell you honey," said one of the women. "That man is mighty fine. She didn't never deserve him anyways. Saggy bosomed turkey neck. Hell bells! She must be about fifty! No one can blame him for checking out the contestants."

"Sneaking into their beach hut for sangria in the hot tub is a bit much. Their bikinis were tiny! I bet the poor woman is mortified," said the other.

Inwardly Casey smiled as he imagined himself in a similar scenario. Only in his version there were no bikinis – only naked skin. Lots and lots of it.

Although he was unable to achieve an erection, he was more than capable of playing out the scenario in his mind as though it were a movie. And with not much else to occupy him, why wouldn't he.?

Steam rose from the writhing bodies as his hands feverishly sought out his giggling companions.

"Mm...yes," murmured one of the girls in his imaginary hot tub. "Faster."

Water splashed everywhere as the action got heavier.

Suddenly a scream rang out.

Casey's pornographic imaginings stopped in mid flow as he spun round to find a woman standing in the corner of his mind with a hand clapped over her mouth. She was staring at the hot tub scene as though she never even knew such things even went on.

Realising she was staring she tried to avert her eyes. But like a compass needle finding north they kept on drifting back to it again.

"Who the fuck are you?" he demanded.

"Don't you speak to me like that you animal, you!" stammered the woman.

"Well who are you? Are you going to tell me or do I have to beat it out of you?" he threatened. He was not happy that he'd been interrupted. They'd just been getting to the best bit.

"There has got to be some kind of mistake," muttered the woman. "God would never let anyone like you become Karma."

She turned to leave thinking that she'd got the wrong guy. That's when Casey realised she was hot. He was so busy eyeing her up he almost missed his chance to stop her.

"Wait!" he called after her.

"What?"

"Are you trying to tell me that God sent you?"

"I've been sent on a mission, yes," the woman replied starchily. "But it would seem there has been a mix up."

Casey grinned.

"Whatever makes you think that?" he said moving in closer.

She turned to look away from his probing stare. He knew he was making her uncomfortable, but it was the only spontaneous interaction he'd had in some time and he was going to milk it for all it was worth.

"Because you're not the kind of person God deals with, that's why." As she said this it occurred to her that he didn't seem overly surprised at what she was saying – and he should have been if it really was a case of mistaken identity.

"Well I happen to think that's all a load of bullshit," Casey shot back.

"Explain," she said.

"Those drugs I took fucked up my brain. You're not real and neither was Karma," he told her. "You're just another figment of my imagination."

"No I'm not! How dare you! This is just insane!"

"No it's not. I can do and say whatever I want," he said breathing heavily. "You're not real."

"Yes I am."

"Prove it then," said Casey folding his arms.

She pouted for a few moments before swallowing her pride. There was nothing else for it she was just going to have to try to convince him who she really was.

"Well, for starters I have a name – Sarah Francis Arellano. And I know things about you that I couldn't possibly know if I wasn't real."

"That's where you're wrong," Casey replied. "If you were a figment of my imagination, you'd know everything I know. The only way to prove who you are is to tell me something I don't know."

"Like what?"

"I dunno," he said shrugging his shoulders. He thought for a minute. "How about – who really killed JFK? Or what really happened at Area 51?"

Sarah gave a tiny snort of derision that she thought he would miss. He didn't.

"What?" he growled. He was getting sick of her disdain.

"Nothing," she shrugged. "Only those are just the sort of questions I'd expect someone like you to come up with."

"Meaning?"

"Meaning there is nothing personal or profound in there. Just your everyday conspiracy theorist nonsense you could turn up in any internet search. Don't you realise the ball is well and truly in your court? You could obtain the answer to any number of questions that have been troubling you personally over the years. Surely even you can come up with something better than that," said Sarah in disgust.

She was making fun at his expense. He didn't like that. Not one bit.

"So you're kinda like my very own genie lamp," he said pressing up against her. His mind appeared to only be half engaged in the current conversation.

"All you need is a couple of rubs," he said leering.

His breath washed over her face as he moved in to taste her skin. Suddenly she vanished and reappeared several feet away. Undeterred, he again advanced on her position with a hungry gleam in his eye.

Sarah had never encountered this kind of behaviour before and although she had the power to evade him indefinitely it still unnerved her greatly.

Back on earth, before her expiration, she had been a nun – confined by not only her vows of celibacy but also the blindness that had afflicted her since childhood. This had shielded her completely from the notion of men hungering for women.

All she had ever known about such things were from brief accounts that had been read to her from the bible – such as David and Bathsheba and Absalom and Tamar.

None of them had been painted in a good light and for a long time she had felt revulsion over the concept of sexual interaction between men and women. In fact, over sexual activity of any kind.

Yet there were times when she found herself curious – wondering what she was missing. After all, God had created such things, so how could they be sinful? Perhaps it had been her lack of sight that made such things beyond her ability to comprehend?

There had certainly been occasions when she had felt strange yearnings in the oddest of places. There was the time when Father Carlos Ramirez was called upon to take Mass for eleven weeks and she had been overtaken by that strange illness.

Being blind she had no idea what Father Ramirez looked like, but she sensed that he was an especially holy man in both appearance and character. But what had really grabbed her attention, was his unbelievably soft hands. So gentle and heart meltingly firm.

During Mass, Sarah was supposed to open her mouth in readiness to accept the sacred wafer that represented Christ's body, just like everyone else. But every time Father Ramirez performed the rites she found herself utterly lost in his voice and as a result she was never prepared.

He never reprimanded her as some of the older priests did. His voice was soothing and he was always gentle and kind. It warmed her in places that it shouldn't have, cocooning her in its deep velvety masculinity. For all she knew he was a fat ugly toad, but deep down she suspected he was not. Not if his voice was anything to go by.

Immersing herself in what he was saying rather than the tone seemed to be the answer. But no matter how hard she tried she just couldn't concentrate – even though she understood Latin.

It was this growing obsession that caused her to forget to open her mouth when kneeling before him for Mass. She was so absorbed in his rough edged baritone and the way it made her feel. The first time it happened she was so surprised when he reached out to part her lips in order to receive the bread that she almost choked to death on it.

Such a paroxysm of coughing took over her body that she had to be escorted to her room where she lay on the bed shaking with tears streaming from her eyes. Their penny pinching Mother Superior was so concerned that she seriously considered calling a doctor. But Sarah assured her that it would pass. And it did, eventually.

That and several other unusual interactions that she had with Father Ramirez left her wondering whether she was ill or falling headlong into the sin of lust.

Now that she was immortal and had gotten the chance to observe, male/female interactions down on planet earth, she realised that she had indeed been falling under the charms of Father Ramirez.

Worse still she had discovered that not only was he devastatingly handsome, but that she herself was in fact considered extremely beautiful.

The very reason why her parents had sent her to the convent to attend school and ultimately join the sister hood, was that they feared that out in the real world she would be preyed upon by men who would take advantage of her lack of sight.

Sarah supposed that she should be thankful that they had tried their best to shield her from men like Casey but somehow in her heart of hearts beneath all the layers of spirituality and indoctrinated righteousness she couldn't help but feel as though she'd been cheated.

Finding out that she was a red hot beauty who wouldn't look amiss in a Hollywood movie seemed like such a waste. She wondered had Father Ramirez noticed her appearance and if it had affected him. But she had no way of knowing. And probably never would.

Right now though, her main problem was that the repulsive specimen she was supposed to be dealing with seemed more than a little attracted to her and she had absolutely no clue what to do about it.

"You really are an animal aren't you?" she scolded.

"You know you want it," Casey said grinding his hips suggestively against her.

Once again she put some distance between herself and Casey.

"That's it!" she cried. "I'm going to have to have a word with God! There is no way on this earth I'm going to have any part in letting you out of here! If it was up to me I'd keep you in here and throw away the key!"

She turned to leave again but he grabbed her by the arm.

"Wait!" he shouted.

She rounded on him with flashing eyes.

"Get your hands off me!"

She suddenly looked convincingly supernatural to Casey. Energy seemed to emanate from her, pushing him away like a force field.

As soon as she had mentioned the possibility of him being released, his mind had switched into full operation and was now focused fully on what she was doing here.

"Look," he said, suddenly letting go of her arm. "I was only winding you up – ok? My days of forcing myself on chicks are over."

Sarah did not look convinced.

"What? Don't they have a sense of humour where you're from?" he chuckled.

She thought briefly about the irony of that. Neither heaven nor the convent where she had formerly lived was known for having peals of laughter ringing through their corridors.

"Rape is never funny," she scolded once again. "You've got a lot to learn."

"Well, before I give in and become your star pupil you're still going to have to convince me, you are who you say you are," he said.

It was tempting to ignore him and just go speak with God but because of her back ground Sarah had great respect for hierarchy – and there was obviously no one higher than God himself.

She had been honoured with a mission and she felt very strongly that she must do everything in her power to fulfil it to the best of her ability.

"You need to come up with a decent question then – one that only a supernatural being could answer," Sarah told him.

"Ok," Casey said. "I've got one."

"Ok, I'm all ears."

"What happened to my mother after the fire?"

Chapter Seven

Who's Who?

THE MOMENT THOSE words had come out of Casey's mouth God convened an emergency meeting.

"Why the hell didn't she just agree to answer the JFK question?" he complained.

Both Gabriel and Nick nodded in agreement. That would certainly have been a lot less problematic. Who knew what this could trigger in someone like Casey?

"Who did the background search on her anyway?" he said flinging a couple of files marked top secret across the desk.

"I think He'vernon did," muttered Gabriel.

"He'vernon? Well that explains it then," God said. "That's the last time we let her have such a position of responsibility. She did a bad enough job training Cal. Now she's messed this up too. Time she was relegated to more menial tasks. From now on she can busy herself looking after the weather systems."

Most people don't know this but God is only all knowing when he chooses to be and even then it can be pretty hit and miss.

A bit like humans on earth choosing whether or not to have a paternity test on their child. They could have that information if they want to, but they may choose not to for various reasons.

Understandably God keeps his finger on the pulse with high profile situations or situations that through experience he recognises as having the potential to become serious or influential to the universal populace. But by enlarge he chooses not to delve into every little aspect of every individual in existence. It was just – well, far too boring.

To be on the safe side he has myriads and myriads of angels who perform random assessments and checks on both earthly subjects and heavenly. Unfortunately from time to time, someone or something slips through the net. Such as Hitler or the Fukushima nuclear disaster.

Those were pretty big events and as such there had been some lengthy disciplinary hearings afterwards. Poor He'vernon had been implicated in those too. Taking the blame seemed to be her lot in life.

"Oh my God!" Gabriel breathed. He was studying the file in front of him with great interest.

"What?" God snapped.

"Sarah is Casey's biological half-sister! She was conceived on the night of the fire, a bi product of Celine's prostitution. Says here she was put up for adoption a couple of hours after her birth. She must not find this out. It would ruin her!"

"Well?" said God, looking across the desk. "How on earth are we going to sort this mess out?"

"We could take her off the case," Gabriel volunteered brightly. "That way she'll never discover her true identity."

Nick frowned. He didn't like that idea.

"No, no. We can't do that. It would raise too many questions amongst the others," God said shaking his head.

"How about we just bump him off? No one would miss him. Problem solved," grinned Gabriel.

Nick didn't look too pleased about that idea either and neither did the boss.

"He can't do that dumbass," Nick sneered. "Everyone knows about God's promise to Karma, that he would train Casey to take up the post once he was gone. Weren't you at the meeting at the Arena of Time?"

"Of course I was!" said Gabriel drawing himself up indignantly. "Least I'm making some kind of contribution here!"

"Come on you two, she's going to be here in a minute!" God said, slamming his fist down on the desk in frustration.

They both jumped. Gabriel paled slightly but the Devil grinned, exposing pointed fangs. He shifted in his chair and leaned forward.

"I have an idea," he said huskily.

"Ok," God answered folding his arms. "I'm all ears."

"I just don't understand why I wasn't told this before," said Sarah after God had explained about the fire that had changed Casey's life forever. "Was anything else left out of the briefing?"

"We told you what we thought was relevant. It wasn't feasible or necessary to tell you everything about Casey."

"Well, with all due respect my Lord, it seems very relevant to me. You want me convince him to take on the role of Karma and then put him through the training program that you and a panel of experts have devised. Don't you think I need to know the subject's background in order to do that?"

"You were told everything that you needed to know Sarah. Simple as that. But the rules have changed somewhat now that he wants to know what happened to his mother."

Sarah tried to appear submissive, but in the back of her mind she wondered if there wasn't another reason why they had withheld this information. It seemed a little odd.

"So what happened to his mother then?" Sarah asked.

"The knowledge of what had happened caused her to lose her grip on reality. She had a complete mental breakdown and to this day has never recovered. No one ever told Casey. He was troubled enough without the knowledge that he had driven his mother crazy too. It's a dangerous game we're playing telling him now really. He's an unstable character at the best of times. In the situation he's in this could really tip him over the edge," God told her gravely. "You must tread carefully."

"I will endeavour to do my best," she promised.

"As soon as possible you must begin his training. Once he shows significant signs of improvement we can put him to the test. Be sure to keep me informed of your progress," God said, bringing the discussion to a close. It really did not feel good misleading her in this fashion but it was necessary. And sure he'd done it with countless millions of religious adherents for millennia.

She nodded her ascent and excused herself praying that she would be able to do a better job this time round. She did not want to disappoint.

Chapter Eight

Mushroom Zombies

DEEP IN THE lush forests of Thailand, Dr Carlos Ramirez was strapped to the trunk of a massive tree taking photographs and video footage of a colony of Carpenter ants. Beneath him was a study platform, capable of taking his weight and more.

The workers who had built at his behest had gone to extreme lengths during its construction to ensure he lived long enough to pay them. It was a sore point with them then that he had also insisted on the extra safety precaution of nylon strapping which tethered him securely to the tree.

The locals who worked for him liked to mock this amongst themselves. But as they conversed in a language he was still struggling to master, he had no idea that his overzealous safety measures were the subject so much derision.

Strangely enough, death and mortality were what preoccupied him of late. It seemed to be inescapable. He gazed down the lens of his hi tech camera, marvelling at the subjects he was studying.

The colony of ants he was observing was infested with a parasitic fungus, one that turned their hosts into mindless zombies and devoured them from the inside out.

This unusual discovery was turning out to be a two edged sword. Not only was it the most unpleasant discovery he had ever made it was also one of the most fascinating - one that would no doubt earn him plenty of column inches in numerous scientific journals. Whilst this discovery was utterly intriguing, there was a certain morbidity to it that triggered a flash flood of troublesome thoughts.

Like many biologist before him who were believers in a higher power, he found himself deeply disturbed by the message nature preached about its maker.

He struggled to reconcile himself to the notion that God had created a parasitic fungus that infested its host then took over its mind for procreative purposes before consuming it from within. The reality was chilling. He knew that from the comfort of a classroom a university student or scholar may view the matter as having little importance but out in the real world the harsh reality of the carpenter ants life cycle was most unpleasant. It was the stuff of horror movies…not that he'd ever seen any.

Carlos watched the tiny ants through his expensive macro lens. They were clearly suffering as they stumbled about with abnormal looking blue/grey eyes. Time lapse photography showed that once the fungus had forced the ant to carry it to a place optimal for its reproductive process, it then killed the host by devouring its brain before sprouting a mushroom from the top of its head. This was to enable it to disperse its spores as widely as possible. He watched in slow motion as the fungus broke through their carapace and burst through the top of their heads. Nature never ceased to amaze him. Or horrify him.

From his youth on he had travelled the world extensively and come across many strange creatures. However this one was the most macabre yet. Their purpose in the grand scheme of things was a puzzle. Surely God had not created such a monstrosity?

Then again, when he looked around at humanity he saw far worse examples of selfish brutality and against their own species too. You could argue that mankind had the capacity for free thinking and that the fungus was genetically programmed to behave in such a manner.

Either way it seemed to him that a perfect God should be expected to create perfect living things – not perfect killing machines, which is in essence what a good deal of life on planet earth in fact is.

He was tempted to put the tiny creature in front of him, out of its misery once he'd finished filming but the lab that had sponsored his expedition wanted live specimens. In his back pack, he had three separate specimen containers housed inside a breathable case. They were very small but had been sent by airmail just for this very purpose. Taking great care not to lose his footing he wrestled his back pack to the front of his body and fished out the miniscule containers.

Carlos expertly flicked three ants into the cylindrical glass chamber and closed the lid. He watched in fascination noting that they immediately began to scurry about, systematically inspecting the glass walls for a way out. Carlos watched the imprisoned bugs with interest, taking note of how soon they concluded their exploration was pointless.

Their size appeared to be no impediment to their intelligence. Carlos admired their apparent logic. He himself had always been a thinker. Born in the slums of Bogota one might think he'd been put at a disadvantage. But for him, thinking had been a way out – an escape.

At first it had provided him with a way to ignore the poverty and violence around him, through imaginative play and then eventually through books and studying. Then as time went on his interests gradually moved towards theology and the Catholic Church. It offered a sense of higher purpose, of being something more than just another piece of human excreta crawling around the shanty towns of Altos de Cazuca.

Although the priesthood beckoned he never lost his interest in biology. At times it warred with his spiritual personage.

In his core, Carlos was a simple man who craved something infinitely rare. Like many others of his kind, Carlos craved the truth.

Many people seek it. Many claim to have found it in some shape or form. But Carlos the man, the thinker, the priest was still searching for answers, which was strange for someone who claimed to be God's spokesperson.

Truth be known, he had yet to cast his vote. But like a good many others he hid his doubt and uncertainty in the ritual of worship.

It was easy to get lost in the glory of the sacred liturgy and the splendid rituals of Catholicism. The masses thrived on the glaring disparity between the multitudinous gilded houses of God and the sprawling slums that housed the general populace alongside a million plague infested rats.

To the average man and woman on the street, Catholicism was right up there with, America and Elvis. To Carlos it was higher still. In his eyes Catholicism and God were one and the same. Intertwined like conjoined twins. Utterly inseparable. So when one fell from grace the other came tumbling after.

Another turning point in his life had been when Sister Sarah Francis Arellano got struck by lightning whilst out walking through the olive groves with two orphans. Up until that point he had been falling hard for her over a period of about three years without even realising it. It was a bit like getting stuck in quick sand.

One day he found himself admiring her beautiful singing voice, the next he was speculating just how soft her cheeks would feel if pressed closely to the stubbly skin of his jaw line. She came to fill his thoughts, in ways that he knew she should not have. A man of God should be able to resist, to draw upon the power of faith. But she was like some kind of precious flower to him. A scarlet poppy in a field of drab corn. An enticing opiate of epic proportions.

The irony was that being blind and brought up in a convent meant that she had no idea how desirable she was to him or any other man. Her delicate beauty was effortless - uncontrived. A God given gift that she would never have call to use.

In the early hours of the morning when he couldn't sleep, he would often lie speculating what she would smell of, the way her hair would fall around his face if he dared ever kiss her.

This always led to pangs of guilt and him having to visit the confession box. There he would tell half-truths and could only hint at his inner torment.

At one point he had to perform Mass in Father Eustace

Rodriguez's stead for several weeks. Which was both a torture and an exquisite pleasure all at the same time. For some reason every time it was Sarah's turn to accept the body of the Christ she forgot to open her mouth. Whether it was because she was blind or because she was just slow Carlos did not know. Either way it drove him crazy.

Every service for weeks on end she just knelt before him and stared up at him with her beautiful unseeing ice blue eyes. Doing his best to ignore her proximity to his throbbing groin, Carlos parted her petal soft lips and pressed the wafer onto her tongue. Always she seemed surprised, expelling a little puff of air from her lungs. It wafted warm and sweet until it released its full exotic potency directly into his flushed face. Holy Father, she was beautiful!

Her death had been an unspeakably painful jolt, and was made worse by the fact that he'd started to get to know her a little better in the preceding months. After looking up the odds of getting hit by lightning on Google and discovering it was estimated to be between one in two hundred thousand and one in a million he decided that she had been the victim of some seriously bad luck. This clashed directly what the priest told those gathered at her funeral. He explained to the flock that although humans may not understand many of the outworking's of Gods purpose everything that happens is the will of God. The implication was that this included Sister Sarah's death.

Instead of seeing it for what it was – a terrible stroke of luck, Father Rodriguez painted it almost as though she had won the lottery. That signalled the start of Father Ramirez's wavering faith. His trip to Thailand was supposed to distract him from such negative thoughts. If he devoted himself to studying the different ant species there his faith may be restored in their maker.

"Go to the ant you lazy one," said Proverbs 6:6.

Well if it was good enough for the lazy one it was good enough for him!

As much as he enjoyed this refreshingly different work, his doubts still kept on bubbling up to the surface.

Once back in his hometown, he further busied himself by setting about writing his findings and for a while he forgot all about the ants that he had sent off to Tresco Labs by airmail. But they were zombie ants and zombies always come back to haunt you.

Chapter Nine

The Tempest

"I'M NOT BUYING it!" announced Casey, looking petulant. Sarah had 'dropped' into his mind once again to answer the question he had posed.

"Look, I know this is difficult to take in, but if you try to think about it from her point of view, she'd had a very traumatic life. Losing her family, such as it was, must have been very hard to take, especially given the circumstances."

Casey understood her meaning and remained silent. He studied the 'floor' at his feet, his thoughts whirling like leaves in the wind.

He closed his eyes and tried to do as Sarah had asked, to put his self in his mother's situation. What must it have been like for her to have to leave her two children with the monster that was their father and return only to find that her son had taken his place? She had handed Josephine his sister over to him, trusting that he would do everything in his power to keep her safe from harm – and look at how he had repaid that trust.

He tried to keep his face a mask of detachment, but he could feel something monstrous trying to get out when he thought of what she had done in order to keep things together. All that had been for nothing in the end. No wonder she had gone crazy.

Once he became an adult and saw that side of life first hand, he knew what she had risked turning tricks to pay for his father's drug habit. He'd seen many a prostitute bleeding and beaten. In fact he himself had made several beg for their lives, back when his anger and hate had ruled him completely.

Underneath that torturer's exterior lay a dark and blackened soul. He was a product of the very thing he'd become. As Sarah watched him struggle with the news of his mother's complete mental breakdown she saw this with far more clarity than the file God gave her could have portrayed. This was something that God would have preferred buried. It was only complicating things further.

It struck her as she watched Casey clutch his knees with white knuckled fists that for all her earthly life she had missed out on an entire human experience. Sight enriched existence in ways that nothing else she had encountered so far could match.

Without sight, had she ever been able to gauge the depth of another person's love, honesty or sadness? This question gave birth to another – a much bigger one – one that she doubted she would receive a satisfying answer to.

Why?

Why had God allowed Sarah to be born blind? Why had he let Casey's mother and father become parents when many much more worthy people remain childless? Sarah had not been dead long, but it was not at all what she had imagined. And neither was

God. Questions that she had not even considered before bubbled away in the back of her mind, simmering like the caldera of a dormant volcano.

She sighed and told herself that in time the answers would come, after all – God is perfect.

Casey looked up at that sound.

"What have you got to sigh about?" he asked.

Sarah fixed him with the most benign expression she could muster.

"It always makes me feel a little sad when I see someone throwing away an amazing opportunity – one that will probably never come their way again."

"I suppose you're going to tell me now how I could do good with what's left of my life and make a difference? What a fucking joke!" he sneered. He was very angry and his voice had a dangerous edge.

"There are things you don't know, Casey, things that would really surprise you if you knew. If only you would show yourself to be a little more humble and ready to change, God may grant you that knowledge in time."

"Oh? Lucky me! What other freaking messed up revelations has he got up his sleeve?" Casey shouted.

Sarah was not used to being spoken to in such a manner and she wasn't sure how to deal with it. She decided to try a firm hand.

"For goodness sake, grow up will you?" she shot back. "What did you expect? A medal? You've spent most of your adult life doing a pretty good impersonation of your father. In fact, you're way worse than he ever was. You're lucky you're not roasting in hell right now, along with…a good many other people."

"Fuck you!" Casey roared, his eyes wide with rage.

They were both losing control.

"I'm a nun. No one ever has and no one ever will!" cried Sarah indignantly. Fear and anger don't mix well together. Like a lit powder keg she was about to go off but Casey couldn't see it. Casey threw back his head and laughed loudly. He was beginning to sound unhinged.

"You're shitting me?"

"No, I am not Mr Davenport, and will you kindly refrain from peppering your speech with expletives. I am quite capable of deciphering your meaning without it!" she spat at him.

"Never been fucked? Well that is something I must remedy then," he breathed demonically, moving purposefully towards her. Reaching out, he grabbed her waist intending to pull her to him.

Far away, in the realms of heaven God, Gabriel and Nick raised their eyebrows at this bold and brazen move. All three watched through the fifty eight inch TV as Sarah finally lost it and hurled Casey's physical body across the hospital room.

With no means to protect himself he fell like a sack of potatoes against the hardwood side table, his head splitting open like an over ripe cantaloupe.

"Shit!" the Devil declared, clapping his hands. He looked thoroughly entertained. "I wasn't expecting that!"

"What is going on here?" God said jumping up out of his chair. The others held up their hands, looking just as confused as he was.

"You!" he said pointing to Gabriel. "Get down there quickly and sort out that mess. I want Sarah back here within the next half hour. She's going to have to answer for this."

Gabriel obeyed immediately, leaving God and Lucifer alone in his office.

"I knew he wouldn't be able to cope with knowing what happened to his mother! Did you know Sarah was going to do that?" asked God in a carefully measured tone.

"Look, I already told you – I wasn't expecting that. And neither were you I take it."

"Whilst it's not common knowledge we both know that the odd one, does slip through the net," admitted God.

"True," nodded Nick. "Guess we'll just have to see if that sissy Gabriel can contain it."

"Care for a cigar while we wait?" God said, casually turning to offer Nick the open box.

"No thanks," replied Nick sardonically. "I don't smoke."

Chapter Ten

Gabriel's Power

BY THE TIME Gabriel arrived, Sarah was long gone. He wasn't sure where she had scurried off to but to be frank that was the least of his worries.

The new Karma was lying on the floor in a pool of blood, his life force slipping away fast. He was surrounded by a trio of humans who were frantically trying to save his life.

Concentrating fiercely on the orb of power that burned within him Gabriel closed his eyes and unleashed the breath that he had been holding. It flowed outwards from him like a magical golden cloud, freezing everything it touched – suspending time itself.

Back in heaven Satan and God sat blinking as the TV screens before them suddenly buzzed with static.

"What's he doing?" God demanded.

"How should I know?" Satan said, a strange smile playing on his lips. "Gabriel always was a wild card."

Back on earth in the hospital room everything glowed with

a strange pallid light. All was deathly still barring Gabriel who strode forward to kneel beside Casey's prone form.

"Ridiculous humans!" he murmured, shrinking from the touch of a frozen nurse at his elbow. "Always getting in the way."

He laid his hands, feather light upon the garish scarlet head wound. He was shocked at how close to death Casey was. Just one more second and he would have been too late. It was going to take a lot to bring him back. He was going to have to do something that he personally had never tried before. Something that he was not entirely sure God would sanction.

His human physicians would have probably attempted to close the lips of the wound but Gabriel knew that things had gone way past that. At his waist hung a bronze and gold short sword forged by God in the heart of a distant sun. It hung from his belt at all times but was usually hidden from view amongst the flowing white linen of his smock.

He withdrew it from its scabbard in one swift move and passed it across both his wrists, swapping it from one hand to the other as he did so. From within the opening of his ghostly flesh a blinding silver white liquid seeped.

It hung suspended for a moment or two before dropping like liquid mercury into the wound on Casey's head. A hiss of steam rose up, almost blinding Gabriel.

From the corner of the room came a gasp.

"What are you doing to him?" Sarah whispered.

"Do not whisper to me from the shadows. Show yourself," said Gabriel wafting away the steam from above Casey's head.

Sarah materialised and came forward nervously. Gabriel gave her a cursory glance before continuing to minister to the subject. She watched as he laid his hands upon his head, not realising that he was directing the scorching hot mercury type substance to the major arteries that had been severed by the shards of bone in his head.

"I said what are you doing?"

Gabriel gave her a withering look over his shoulder.

"I am attempting to repair the damage that you have done."

Sarah had always been in awe of Gabriel and could think of no fitting response.

"You'd better hope that I can save him. There is a good deal hanging in the balance here as you well know," he said gravely.

Sarah nodded. She knew that a new Karma was required and that God had made a promise that must be kept. For what seemed like an eternity she let Gabriel work unhindered, hoping that he could indeed pull off the miracle that was required.

Eventually he stood up and stretched.

"Done!" he said.

"You did it?"

"I did what I could. Now we have to see if his body will respond and of course there's no telling what those medical idiots will pump into him. I've seen it happen before. One of us comes down here, spends an age bringing someone back from the brink of death only for the medical profession to screw it up. If you hadn't messed up so badly I'd leave you here to keep watch over him. But no can do. The big man wants to see you," he said.

That made Sarah's heart pound. She knew that she had made a serious error. Losing control like that was not supposed to happen now that she was immortal. She had lashed out, which was a very human reaction and almost killed a very important person in the grand scheme of things.

Yes, God had every right to be angry with her she thought anxiously. The only option open to her was to go back and face the music. Apprehension niggled away at her due to her uncertainty of what the outcome would be. She had rarely heard of immortals being punished for misdemeanours and when they had it had never, ever turned out well.

Usually it involved banishment of some sort or imprisonment in the black pits of Tartarus – a place of absolute sensory deprivement – a place of isolation, where only thought exists. In fact it was a lot like the situation Casey had been in.

That troubled her a lot that she may be perceived as having sunk to his level in that she had almost killed another human being and could therefore be worthy of such a judgement.

How it had happened was beyond her. She could safely say she'd never had a violent bone in her body before today. He seemed to trigger something in her. Something utterly primal. A fear that she had never even known before. He had so much rage within him.

The thought that a man like him could think of her in that way, of doing those things to her as though she was some sort of disposable crack whore angered her *and* it also made her afraid.

And let's face it, life on the spiritual plain was not what she had imagined it would be. God was not what she imagined him to be.

There were times when she felt unsure of his feelings towards mankind. She was beginning to see him as being detached from the reality of what was going on down on earth.

The moment Casey had threatened to violate her, even though it was impossible, she felt doubtful as to whether God would have intervened. That too had angered her.

She would have to try and banish these negative emotions before she was called before him.

"Can I trust you to make you own way back to heaven then? Or do I have to escort you myself?" Gabriel asked.

This shocked her. More than ever she felt like a criminal.

"Yes. Of course," she said humbly.

"Be on your way then," he said nodding his head.

Without a word she made her way back to heaven, stumbling along the ancient stairway. Unsure of what to expect she knocked timidly on God's large mahogany office door and waited.

Chapter Eleven

Fortune Favours the Bold

THE MAN STANDING trial was handsome, with a square manly jawline, a strong nose and proud features. He twirled a jet black moustache as he studied the pretty Spanish security guard standing to the side of a heavy set of doors. His eyes twinkled as he fantasized about what he would do to her, given half the chance.

The medals he had won, supposedly for feats of great valour on behalf of Bosnia, his native country swung gently above his left breast. That had been a good many years ago. Times had changed a greatly since then.

But Zdravko Blasevic had not. He was still devilishly handsome and he was still the monster that had inspired fear amongst thousands for almost a decade.

"The prosecution calls to the stand our main witness – Franjo Susak," announced a balding middle aged general.

A pronounced hush fell as a withered old man was led into the room. The smell of death and old age clung to him like dampness saturating the leaves of a forest floor in autumn.

He hobbled over to the stand and was sworn in by the clerk.

"So who is this guy then?" Casey asked.

He and Sarah were observing the trial from the empty upper gallery.

"He is the sole survivor of the Dradtzoja massacre," whispered Sarah. "He lost everyone he had ever known the day that Zdavko Blasevic's men walked into his village."

"Please be seated," said the judge, motioning for him to sit down.

He complied with great dignity, carefully perching a pair of gold rimmed spectacles on his stubby little nose.

Once he had settled himself comfortably the prosecution began to cross examine him. Gently at first but soon the questions became more difficult as they probed into the past, a place that eighty nine year old Franjo did not like to go any more.

In a voice that crackled like sticks under foot he told how Zdravko Blasevic's troops had poured into Dradtzoja on June the twenty ninth, raping, pillaging and murdering their way through the village.

In a voice that belied his inner turmoil he told the court how he had been held at gun point and forced to watch the soldiers repeatedly gang rape not only his elderly sister but also his wife and daughter.

Afterwards he had been forced to dig their graves. Then one by one they were lined up and shot at point blank range. Zdravko's men started to cover their bullet riddled bodies with dirt but were rudely interrupted by a UN peacekeeping force landing just outside the village. Although much too late, they began laying down heavy fire in an effort to flush the enemy out.

In the midst of all this Franjo had somehow survived the attack and lay bleeding in the freezing snow. Even whilst frostbite was eating away at his limbs the snow proved to be his ally by helping the blood coagulate and slow his heartbeat. As the Russian field doctor had put it when he was dumped unceremoniously on his operating table,

"Lie with the snow when you're drunk and it will freeze your hairy ball sack off. Lie with the snow when you're dying and it might just save your life."

He went on to tell him, "It's a lot like my former mistress, Bianca the ice queen. She was also bewitchingly beautiful and she unwittingly saved my life by stabbing me in the back. If she hadn't done so the surgeons would never have discovered the aggressive tumour taking over my liver, so I forgive her."

The crazy Russian field doctor had lifted up his tunic and showed him the brutal scarring.

"See? The wounds of love," he had laughed.

As Franjo had drifted in and out of consciousness the doctor told him how Bianca his mistress had given him the worst ultimatum a man could have. Give up the drink or else no sex. It had led to a huge row between them during which she stabbed him. He had told him this tale to keep him conscious. It was the only way he would know whether or not he was damaging the speech centre in his brain.

It was at this stage that Franjo Susak had begged the doctor to stop operating on him and just let him die. He was experiencing very little in the way of physical pain. His pain, as he put it, "was that of a broken and savaged heart."

He started to resist the doctor's ministrations with what

little strength he had left.

"Let me go!" he pleaded weakly.

The nurse who had been helping the doctor threw up her hands in despair and left the room. But the doctor would not give up. He gripped his patient roughly by the shoulder and leaned down to whisper,

"God has spared you for a reason my friend. You *must* survive to bring this monster to justice."

Since that day Franjo had endured seven further operations to correct the horrendous damage done by the bullets that had torn through his body. Every single one had weakened him but he had been determined to hang on until this day – the day he faced his nemesis in court.

As the two men looked at each other across the court room it became apparent that something was wrong. Part way through Franjo's testimony his breath turned to ragged gasps.

Zdavko's eyes glittered brightly like chips of polished jet as he watched the old man sink to his knees.

"Get a medic in here now!" barked the judge.

Within seconds a team of trained doctors knelt beside him as the assembled courtroom watched and held their breath.

"So what happens now?" Casey said turning to Sarah.

"Shhh!" said Sarah severely. "We must wait and see."

His condition was serious, forcing the judge to dismiss those assembled. Only a few carefully selected individuals were allowed to remain: Franjo's legal team, the medics, a highly trained security detail and the judge.

"He's not going to make it," said Casey in disgust. "So much for God sparing him."

"Who's up there?" called the judge, looking up into what should have been an empty gallery.

Although he could not see Sarah and Casey, he'd heard a smattering of the comments Casey had made. Immediately the security team dashed up the stairs in search of the intruder. They fanned out, waving flash lights into every darkened corner, weapons at the ready.

Of course they found nothing. Another sound broke the silence. It was the whine of a defibrillator charging.

"Clear!" said one of the medics. Leaning forward he applied the paddles in an effort to jump start Franjo's broken heart. A dull thump could be heard and the old man's body twitched in a lifeless manner. For forty five minutes they shocked his heart but to no avail.

"Time of death, eleven twenty two," said a female medic, checking her watch. With the gentlest of fingers she closed his eyes as those in the room gazed down at him solemnly.

"Well I suppose that's it then," said Franjo's lawyer dabbing his forehead with a handkerchief. "Without him we don't have much of a case."

"You've nothing else to present? What about forensic evidence or surveillance?" said the judge frowning. He hated the thought of the general getting away with the atrocities he'd committed.

"The most persuasive evidence we had was Franjo's testimony. Everything hinged on that. We do have some ballistic evidence and some satellite surveillance your honour. But nothing conclusive that would be enough to put him away for as long as he deserves," said the lawyer.

"Then the trial will collapse and I'll have no choice but to throw the case out and release the general," sighed the judge.

This was not what he wanted at all. He was due to retire at the end of the year and he had wanted his career to end on a high note. The way things were looking it was very probable that it would be more like a quiet fizzle.

"Let's be perfectly candid here your honour, neither you or I wants that to happen. But at this moment in time our options are very limited. You can either throw the case out of court due to lack of evidence or…"

"Or what?" said the judge.

"Or you could grant us an extension. Time to 're-evaluate' the case let's say. You don't need to package it that we're trying to gather more evidence against him. That would put his people on alert and curtail any potential leads. Anything incriminating could just disappear into thin air if we do that. Would you be willing to give us more time?" asked the lawyer hopefully.

He knew he was going out on a limb here asking the judge in such an informal setting but hopefully it would work in their favour and the judge would feel less pressured than if he'd been asked in open court.

"You know my hands are tied. If I'm seen to be giving you too big an extension then it will be obvious to people what's going on. I think the most I can give you is two or three days as the official stand will be that you need to re-evaluate your case after losing your key witness," the judge said. "I'll reconvene the court this afternoon at which time you may ask for an extension in an official capacity. I'm sure it goes without saying that you must act discreetly and that there must be absolutely no mention of this conversation."

"Of course your honour," nodded the lawyer. "I thank you for your understanding."

"Don't mention it," said the judge, holding his gaze.

The two men parted company and left the medics to their work. Up in the gallery Casey and Sarah were now alone, the security detail having made a thorough sweep of the area and had left.

"What a screwed up fucking mess!" whispered Casey.

Sarah sucked her breath in through her teeth and tried to overlook the fact that Casey had once again used profane speech.

"Yes it is a mess and it's up to us to clean it up," she told him matter of fact as though they were talking about a messy kitchen or something equally trivial.

"I don't mean that!" he exclaimed far too loudly. The medics down below looked up suspiciously having heard the echoes from his outburst. But they were far too busy making records and making arrangements with the coroner. They just shrugged and continued with their job.

"I mean it's really screwed up that you expect me to go and judge this guy or whatever it is that Karma is supposed to do. You do know that if it wasn't for my 'little accident' I'd probably be out doing just the sort of things that I'm supposed to be judging this guy for."

"Are you saying that it's just because you're physically unable to do those things that's preventing you?" asked Sarah. Her dark eyebrows were deeply furrowed as she struggled to understand him.

"Not exactly, no," he said defensively.

"So what's changed then?"

"You're missing the point here," he said sounding frustrated.

"Ok, ok," said Sarah holding up her hands. "But promise you'll talk some more about that later?"

Casey rolled his eyes and said nothing. Sarah folded her arms, unwilling to let him avoid the issue.

"Alright fine!" he sighed.

"Good!" said Sarah triumphantly. "Now let's go back to what you were saying. You don't feel as though you're worthy to judge Zdravko?"

"That's not what I was saying at all! What I meant was that it was really out of whack me judging him when I'm not much better than him myself. What right do I have?" demanded Casey.

"You have every right. A God given right. God gave you the position of Karma so he must know that you are worthy and that you're more than capable of doing the job," she told him patiently. "Well he must know things about me that I don't then."

"Of course he does! God knows everything," Sarah explained feeling a slight twinge of doubt niggling away in the back of her mind.

Casey just laughed loudly in her face. It didn't really matter now anyway as there was no one left in the room. The coroner had been in while they were talking and had taken away the body.

"Aww…you religious people are always so gullible," he said shaking his head and laughing.

"Don't give me that!" said Sarah indignantly. "You know full well that there is a higher power at work. You've seen the evidence. For goodness sake, I am the evidence. We both are!

How do you think we got here? How do you think you survived that head injury?"

"Ok. I have to admit that there does seem to be a supernatural force at work," he admitted. "Maybe there is a God after all. Who knows? If so my question is this – what sort of God is he?"

"What do you mean?" said Sarah dubiously.

"I mean what sort of God is he to allow stuff like this to be going on? You talk as though he's infallible and knows everything. But I see no evidence of that."

"Stop right there," snapped Sarah. "Don't you think you should have a little gratitude after everything he's done for you? If it wasn't for him you wouldn't even exist. None of us would. If it wasn't for him you would have died on the floor in that hospital ward. Your head was crushed like an eggshell. And to be painfully honest I think if you had you would have been getting exactly what you deserved."

"Exactly!" said Casey triumphantly. "You think he made a mistake in letting me live. You just said so. I think there are lots of other people who would agree. Yet he did spare me. According to you he sent Gabriel to heal me. Now here I am being asked to inflict Karma on somebody who trained a whole army of guys to behave the way I did. That is pretty screwed up, you've got to admit."

"Just because it doesn't make sense to us immediately doesn't mean that he's made an error in judgement. He knows the big picture. He knows how things will ultimately turn out. God always knows what to do for the best."

"Well, I don't buy that either. Obviously life was pretty fucking peachy for you, locked away in your ivory tower at the convent. But in case you hadn't noticed life doesn't always work out that way for everyone. In some cases it's Hell on earth. But you wouldn't know anything about that, would you?" snapped Casey.

That last comment stung Sarah. She took a deep breath to compose herself before responding.

"Look," she sighed. "I know you had a raw deal. And I'm sorry for that. Lots of people do. It's a fact of life. Perhaps that's why God's letting you have another chance, because you didn't have a fair start in life? Who knows? I don't claim to have all the answers. My faith fills in the gaps."

Casey snorted.

"Listen, it's not constructive to argue like this. We have to focus on the task set before us. We can't let Zdravko get away with his misdeeds. He has to pay."

"No! You listen!" said Casey sharply. "If you want me to do your dirty work for you, you're going to have to give me some decent answers."

A part of Casey's mind registered shock that he was going after this with such vehemence.

He'd never cared much about things of a spiritual nature before. It was as though questions of a profound nature had lay hidden underneath his violent semi-psychopathic nature all this time.

He wondered briefly if that hadn't been partly what fuelled his rage - that he had no answers.

It didn't look like he was going to be getting any, any time soon either. This woman was nothing more than a drone, programmed to follow by indoctrination.

"I'll see what I can arrange. But in the mean time we have to take care of Zdravko," said Sarah. "Have we got a deal?"

"Deal!" he said holding out his hand.

Chapter Twelve

Desperado

FATHER RAMIREZ HOISTED the rucksack higher up onto his shoulder. As small as it was, it carried all his earthly possessions; a spare pair of shoes, another set of clothes, a bible, three photographs, a wallet and a water bottle.

He'd filled that just before he'd said goodbye to everyone at the convent and he was glad that he had done so for the weather was dry and very, very hot. Already he was parched after spending only minutes at the bus stop.

The heat shimmered above the dusty road. Away in the distance he could see the bus making its way towards him. Soon it would take him on the first leg of his journey – away from this place that had lately become such a source of unhappiness.

His destination lay almost two thousand miles away on the outskirts of Mexico City.

As he journeyed there he hoped to help as many people as possible in whatever way he could, in the process restoring his own faith in God's goodness. It had taken quite a knock over the last year or so but he was determined to overcome this temporary crisis by focusing on others instead of himself.

The time had come to throw himself on the mercy of God.

Chapter Thirteen

The Meeting

"ACCORDING TO THE world's leading astronomers 2013 looks set to be the year of the comet, the most notable being the comet Ison, discovered only in September this year by astronomers Vitali Nevski and Artyom Nevichonok. During the months of November and December it will be clearly visible, shining brighter than a full moon," the newscaster said brightly.

Zdravko Blasevic shifted in the comfortable bed inside his high security prison cell, tucking the soft blanket underneath his stubbly chin.

He grinned to himself as he wondered where he would be this time next year – probably watching the comet fall across the sky on the sands of some far away exotic beach. He knew that the trial would fall apart now. His defence team had told him so.

They had very little else on him. No witnesses had been left. Any evidence they had was shaky at best. There was simply not enough to make a solid conviction.

Now that old man Franjo was dead they'd be forced to

release him but not only that they would have to compensate him. His team would make sure of that.

The absurdity of it amused him. Given half the chance he would do it all again. In his opinion those days had been the best of his career. Hell, they'd been the best of his life.

"They were not the best days of your victims lives though, were they?" said a voice.

Zdravko sat up sharply, bumping his head against the overhanging bunk. He cursed loudly.

"Who said that?" he called out rubbing his head. "Show yourself!"

"There is nothing to show," whispered a hollow rustling voice. "I am a spirit, sifting through the thoughts in your head."

"I don't believe you!" rumbled the general sceptically.

"Have it your way," said the voice dripping with sarcasm. Suddenly a door way opened up in the cell wall behind him. He turned in horror as a great wave of heat and flames poured out. Skeletal hands clawed at his clothes, dragging him slowly in. He clung to the bunk for all he was worth, kicking and screaming in defiance.

"Not so great being on the other side of the fence is it?" something or someone breathed into his face.

The breath felt hot. Hotter than the flames licking at his feet. He had a sneaking suspicion who it belonged to.

"Please don't send me there!" he begged. "I don't deserve to spend an eternity in hell!"

From anyone else such pleading would have been pitiful. But Casey and Sarah had seen and heard what he had done. The two of them had watched an old man who'd lost everything give his last breath in an effort to convict him for the horrific crimes he had perpetrated against his countrymen and women.

"We'll be the judge of that," cackled Casey. His demonic laugh echoed around the cell. Zdravko desperately hoped someone would hear and save him.

"Help! Help!" he shouted.

But no one could hear. Casey and Sarah had made sure of that.

The Devil appeared in the fiery door way and pulled him inside with one mighty tug. Once inside he grabbed him by the throat. Flashing his teeth he grinned fiendishly,

"Welcome to my world," he said.

Just as the door closed Sarah and Casey heard the general give an ear piercing scream. It was enough to make Sarah's blood run cold, if she'd had any.

"I don't know how you came up with that," said Sarah, once everything had returned to normal.

"Well, it just seemed like the best option. I didn't want to kill him. Just scare him witless. Give him a taste of his own medicine."

"It's so ironic though giving him a nightly vacation in hell, especially when he was just thinking about an exotic holiday," said Sarah shaking her head in amusement.

"Yeah well, it's not real. Just a product of his own subconscious after a little creative tinkering by the Devil and I. He'll be as right as rain when he wakes up. Until tomorrow night…"

"Well I think God's going to be pleased with today's work," she said smiling. "You're shaping up pretty well for a guy from the wrong side of the tracks."

"Women!" complained Casey. "One minute they're being all sentimental over you the next they're bashing your fucking head in!"

That took the smile of Sarah's face. She still hadn't gotten used to his bad language and he still hadn't managed to tone it down.

"What have I told you about…?" began Sarah. But she didn't get to finish the last part of that sentence. Filling the bottom left hand corner of the TV screen was the picture of a man. A priest. Apparently he was missing and had last been seen in Mexico City trying to ease the plight of the street children.

"Father Carlos Ramirez came to the city from his home town of Altos de Cazuca hoping to help those less fortunate than himself. It is estimated that Mexico City alone has almost two million underprivileged and homeless street children many of whom are orphans on account of the growing Aids epidemic. Life on the street for a child in Brazil is extremely dangerous with reports circulating of vigilante death groups forming to rid the streets of them earning as much as fifty dollars for each child killed and even police involvement in countless murders every year. Shocking facts indeed!" said the news broadcaster.

Sarah stared at the screen aghast.

"But what is even more shocking," continued the presenter. "Is that Father Ramirez is an eminent and highly respected biologist who just recently made extraordinary discoveries in that very field. Yet this man chooses instead to live a selfless life, dedicated to God and the helping of others. We're now going to interview Dan Stevens, scientist and former colleague at the Stansted Institute."

She turned to face a bearded man sitting to her left.

"Are we going to go now or what?" said Casey interrupting. "Not that I'm in any hurry to be back in that flesh and blood prison cell you understand."

"Shhh…" sister Sarah admonished him, still glued to the screen.

"Ok!" sighed Casey plumping himself down on the bed right next to the still sleeping general, who was twitching like a cat in his sleep.

"So Professor Stevens, what sort of man would you say Father Ramirez is and what would you like to say to anyone who may be holding him captive against his will or who may know his general whereabouts?"

"Obviously I would encourage anyone with such knowledge to come forward. He is a man of extraordinary courage, intelligence and great character. He has an intense love of the natural world. An inquisitive and enquiring mind which was no doubt responsible for his numerous discoveries and scientific papers," the man said.

The presenter leafed through her notes briefly.

"I believe he had specific difficulty with his most recent discovery…the so called zombie ant of the rain forests," she said, doing her best to probe a little deeper. Her interviewee squirmed in his chair as a short time lapse clip ran of the zombie ant's behaviour.

"I believe it did raise certain issues that were especially troublesome to him, being a man of the cloth."

"Do you believe this has anything to do with his disappearance?"

"I cannot say. But he is the truest man I ever met, that much I can tell you. I hope that he is returned to us safe and well...and soon."

"Indeed. Thank you for joining us today in the studio. And of course if anyone has any information on the whereabouts of Dr Ramirez they can call this number at the bottom of the screen," the newsreader told her viewers.

"Carlos," murmured Sarah.

"You know him?"

"Once," she replied. "Come on!"

She took him by the arm and opened up a dimensional tear with her left hand. It glimmered silver and gold as she dragged him through to the other side.

"Wait!" cried Casey. "Where are you taking me?"

He stared at the celestial staircase throbbing with untold power. This was not a place he recognised and he was not sure he wanted to go there.

"God wants to see you."

"Oh."

By now he believed in the existence of God or a God but that did not automatically translate into him wanting to meet him. He tried not to show just how much this latest news disconcerted him. It sounded pretty ominous even to a hard case like him.

His powers were still limited. He could not shift through dimensions without the aid of Sarah or other celestial beings. Therefore there was only one choice left open to him.

Casey Davenport, former thief, murderer and rapist, followed Sarah, the blind ex-nun, up the stairs as they made their way to an audience with God.

Heaven was a curious place. It was a lot like Casey had imagined it to be yet there were oddities that bemused him. Things that seemed out of place that stood out like a sore thumb. Such as the glass skyscrapers that lay partially hidden behind walls of stationary clouds. Then there were the pure gold statues of various deities and the pale blue crystalline trees that lined a singular avenue that stretched away into the distance as far as the eye could see.

Casey frowned at the sight of a little wizened black man trimming the trees with an electric strimmer. It all seemed a bit odd to say the least. But what did he know about such things?

Sarah leaned in and said quietly,

"A lot of what you see here is metaphorical. They represent things that are difficult or impossible to understand from our limited point of view. So our mind translates them into the closest approximation it can manage. In a nut shell, things are not as they actually appear."

"No shit," said Casey sarcastically.

Sarah clamped a hand around his mouth.

"P*lease* do *not* swear in heaven!" she hissed forcefully.

"Sorry," he said with a casual shrug. "I always swear more when I'm stressed."

"There is no need to be stressed," said rich baritone voice from behind them.

Casey jumped.

"My Lord!" said Sarah, her eyebrows almost grazing her hairline. She hoped he hadn't overheard all of their conversation.

"Calm down," he said in mild reproof. "I'm the Almighty, not an ogre."

Casey's shifted nervously from one foot to the other.

"Come!" God ordered, clicking his fingers. "We need to talk."

Just like that they were transported to his immense office where God seated himself in an ergonomically shaped soft leather chair. Before his desk Casey and Sarah stood like two naughty children waiting anxiously to hear what he had to say.

He leafed idly through a file marked *Zdravko Blasevic*.

"It would seem you are both to be commended. I can see this has been a very successful mission. Zdravko has already shown signs of character modification, partly due to the karma and partly because of the treatment he is now receiving at the mental asylum," God said.

"Mental asylum?" echoed Sarah. "What mental asylum?"

"Yes," said God folding his hands upon the desk. "It would seem that he came back from his night trip to the Hell dreamscape quite deranged. Been there for the last two weeks, Gabriel says."

"Serves him right," said Casey.

God smiled at him in a fatherly manner.

"Well, you've certainly taken to the job very well I must say. You're predecessor was right to recommend you for it."

"Thanks."

"Don't mention it. I'm a big believer in giving praise where it's due," he smiled.

"Who was he? My predecessor, if you don't mind my asking," Casey said. He was seizing the opportunity to ask while the going was good.

"You can ask all you want, but I'm afraid I'm not at liberty to say. It doesn't work like that. Each Karma must remain disconnected from the one previous. Keeps things simple."

"Oh. Ok."

"But I can tell you who your next case will be," he said handing Casey a bulky file.

It was marked *Fernando Cortez*. He was the chief of police in Xochimilco, a district of Mexico City. The file contained information on his habits, personal history, weaknesses, his fears and of course his misdemeanours, which were lengthy.

It was a vile catalogue of corruption ranging from, abuse of power, racketeering, collusion with drug cartels, involvement in the sex trade and worst of all the torture and murder of countless street children.

"Wooah! This guy is a real dirt bag!" exclaimed Casey scanning through the pages.

"Takes one to know one," muttered Sarah. It just slipped out without her meaning it to.

Casey glared.

"Enough!" said God raising his voice slightly.

The very sound of it made the hairs stand up on the back of Casey's neck.

"Sometimes I tire of all this…" God muttered running his fingers through his steely hair. He turned away to scrutinize the countless TV screens hanging from the wall.

Sarah and Casey looked at each other in confusion. Surely God did not mean what they thought he did? Disinterest and apathy were human emotions. Not something they expected to be troubling Almighty God.

"Do you want me to go with him again?" Sarah called out. Her voice echoed around the vast room.

It seemed to irritate God.

He made a strange gesture, almost as if he was catching the errant echo and was crushing it flat like a tin can between his palms. The echo was no more. What had become of it nobody knew – except God.

"There is no need to raise your voice in order to be heard by me, child," he said kindly. "I have the power to hear all humans, no matter where they are if I so wish."

"Well why don't you then?" Casey said before he could stop himself. Freeness of speech must be quite contagious up in heaven he decided.

God chuckled quietly to himself as though they'd shared a private joke.

"Don't be ridiculous!" he laughed.

"It is not for us to question the Lords ways," Sarah interjected quickly. She shot Casey a warning glance.

"I should be pleased to assist him in bringing karma to Fernando, if you will allow it," she said with a brief bow of her head.

Her deference to his lofty position pleased him.

"It does please me…" he said with a slow nod. "But not half as much as my three o clock massage. Henri is due any minute."

As if on cue, a stereotypical Swedish masseuse appeared, poking his head round the door and holding an armful of hot fluffy towels.

"Come in Henri. These two are just leaving," said God stretching out on a soft beige leather treatment couch that had just appeared from the ether. He'd already stripped naked. The only things sparing his modesty were the magnificent shimmering wings that were folded neatly against his back.

Casey and Sarah filed out sheepishly, carefully averting their eyes as they went.

"You know what to do," said the Lord, his mouth and nose protruding through the convenient breathing hole in the treatment couch.

"Make him pay!" he called.

"We will," they said closing the door behind them.

Chapter Fourteen

Papa

WHEN HE WAS out of earshot they referred to him as their Granddad or Papa although they knew full well that he was not. Juan was nobodies Granddad that they knew of. He had no connections out in the real world of bricks and mortar houses, lawns and semi- automatic motor cars. A dark, hopeless, shambolic figure, it was clear to all that life had cast him off and that like a good many others he had fallen through the gaps.

He was a reject of society. Devoid of any value and dignity. Should he have been run over by a car he would not even have been counted worthy of a second glance, much like the alley cats that the children often saw pasted wafer thin on the asphalt.

Life was cheap in Mexico City. Even for an old man. Even for little kids. For that reason, the rejects tended to stick together. For security.

The concept of security was a lot like the tooth fairy or Santa to the street kids of Mexico City. It was a cuddly ideal to cling to in the hours before sleep arrived, when you were gripped by the pangs of hunger or drug withdrawal or recovering from a particularly vicious beating. It always helped if you could think of a place where security might be an actual bonafide reality or some imaginary existence where you were lucky enough to attain it.

That's what street children do – long for that sacred Nirvana. But it never comes – least not for the vast majority.

Up until now Ricardo and Maria were no different. But that didn't stop them from chasing shadows. Thus is the nature of the human spirit.

"We must improve our strategy," Juan said to them gravely one day.

"And it is about time we changed our area," Maria nodded. She was seven, almost eight and not much bigger than a grasshopper.

She climbed up on Juan's knee and played with his filthy beard. His body odour was enough to make a person's eyes water even from a distance for it had been a good part of a decade since he had bathed. Still, she laid her head affectionately on his shoulder. Either she had no sense of smell or she pure and simple did not care.

"Any suggestions?" Juan asked, flicking away a bothersome fly. His other arm was wrapped around her tiny shoulder in an absently protective gesture.

"Let's go to the Teirra Del Fuego Market place and try for some of that fruit. It looks so delicious," Ricardo said licking his lips a little.

"There will be water melon," murmured Maria. Her eyes were as big as saucers as she remembered the sweet pink juicy flesh with its generous speckling of dark oval pips. It had always been her dream to taste one.

"Getting our hands on one of those would be no easy task," Ricardo said bringing her back down to the earth with a thump.

He saw her disappointment and tried to make it up to her. This was not a trivial issue. It was a big deal to Maria.

"But I will try my very best to get one for you. Failing that I'll go for a freshly picked coconut. How does that sound?"

She nodded without looking up. The market place was scary. Lots of big farmers hung around there. She didn't want either of them taking risks. Not for her. All the way to the piazza the thought of it troubled her. It was much too risky. They could be killed! As they neared the merchant's quarter her inner conflict became all too much.

"I'm not that hungry," she cried, tugging on their wrists.
"Silly little Maria!" scolded her brother. They both walked on regardless.

Panic swamped her as she watched them casing the stalls. Other street children were there too, dodging in and out of doorways and searching through rubbish that had been cast aside, hoping to find a tasty morsel or two. The smell was just too tempting to ignore as it held the promise of a full stomach. For the moment her unease subsided as she stood and sniffed, shoulders drawn back. She sighed deeply upon finding the air richly flavoured with the aroma of roasted coffee beans, fruit, leather, bread and spices. Some of the stalls sold hot food as well – mostly filled corn tortillas, skewered meat, tacos and the like. It made Maria's mouth water.

"*Vete a la chingada*!" screamed a fat woman dressed in brightly coloured woven dress. She barrelled out from behind the market stall she was tending and chased after a group of street kids. They'd taken food from her stall and were now hurriedly stuffing their faces with it as they scampered away. She had no hope of ever catching up. Undeterred and morally outraged by their brazenness she grabbed the nearest object to her and used it as a missile.

The can of black eyed peas went arcing through the air, spinning prettily as it went. The fat woman had some size throwing arm and had invested considerable power into this action. Ordinarily her aim was completely hopeless but rage had improved her accuracy tenfold.

With a resounding whack the tin of beans caught one of the fleeing children a glancing blow and he fell to the ground lifelessly. The other children knew better than to hang around.

"Fetch Senior Cortez," the woman implored the crowd. "He will teach this little rat a lesson he won't forget in a hurry."

The name Cortez inspired fear amongst the street dwellers. Whilst in the spot light of the local media he was a man of semi heroic deeds. A charitable sort willing to stand up for the common man and woman. Unfortunately, the street dwellers were not classed as commoners in Mexico City. They were beneath that. They were classed along with the vermin that haunted the back alleys and sewers.

As the chief of police in Xochimilco he had to be careful though. In public he ran a thin line between oppression and tolerance of the city's homeless. His official line was that they must be regulated and monitored, as though they were a species of animal out on the savannah threatening the existence of another. In reality he addressed 'the problem' with organised regular culling of the street rats through death squads that roamed the streets. He paid those men as much as fifty US dollars for every child they killed. The general populace did not know this because he made sure that the trail of broken bodies could not be traced back to him. He would appear on television and wring his hands for *'the poor, poor cheeldren'* making fervent promises to find the culprits. No one ever did and few people really cared anyway.

So at the very mention of Fernando Cortez Maria's blood ran cold. She slipped away just as a tall man dressed in priests robes arrived on the scene.

"Give the child to me," she heard him say. *Wow! He sounded just like Jesus!*

Whatever else was said was drowned out by the noise of those gathered. Thankfully, the place was getting quite busy, enabling her to disappear into the crowd unnoticed.

"There you are Maria!" said Ricardo pulling her to one side.

She shrieked as she was still feeling jumpy after what had happened to the other little boy.

He looked at her curiously.

"What's the matter with you?" he asked.

"Nothing," she lied. "I'm fine."

"Good," he said with a nod. "You should be. Juan and I are about to get you that water melon."

Instead of happiness a sense of foreboding crept along her spine.

"No brother. I don't need it. I will find us some scraps. Maybe that lady on the fish stall will give us a few heads again if no one is looking."

He pursed his lips and frowned thinking her ungrateful.

Before she could explain otherwise a loud crash came from one of the many colourful stalls.

"There he goes…," said Ricardo. "That's my signal."

"Be careful," Maria begged.

He moved off towards the commotion and she began to wish she'd never mentioned that stupid water melon! Aware of her reservations he turned and winked. She returned his smile but could not feel it. As he was the eldest she felt obligated to trust his judgement but her fear of losing him wouldn't be stilled.

The source of the almighty crash was now apparent. A crowd had assembled to watch an old man who had fallen against a fruit stand and was now thrashing around on the floor. They chattered excitedly, pointing and gesticulating as they tried to figure out what was the matter.

"What is wrong with him Mama?" asked a little boy.

"Drunk most likely or else possessed," she told him with a sniff.

Hearing their comments pleased the old man. Feeling that he was indeed doing an excellent job Juan decided that in spite of his arthritic hips he must pour his heart and soul into it. In an effort worthy of an Oscar he jerked and frothed at the mouth scattering the crowd with his flailing limbs.

Meanwhile Ricardo kept watch on the stall owner who happened to be an unfortunately vigilant man. Whilst he was curious about what was going on, he seemed unwilling to take his eye off the stall. Either he was suspicious by nature or he had learnt the hard way. Before long this problem came to Juan's attention also despite his absorption in his role. He could see it was going to take a bit more innovation on his part to get what they were after.

Suddenly he started babbling loudly in addition to his vigorous thrashing about and grimaces. Most of it was just random nonsense but every now and then he threw in a quasi-religious word or phrase. He knew how superstitious his country men and women were.

The effect was immediate. Everyone in the group began crossing themselves, convinced that they were seeing someone in the throes of a violent demon possession.

His eyes rolled up into the back of his head and he lashed out hard with his arms and legs. A woman screamed loudly as he caught her with a swift kick to the shins.

The fruit stall owner looked up and a water melon disappeared from the pile behind him. Sitting beneath the cotton cloth that covered the stall Ricardo looked down at his prize and grinned. It wasn't in his nature to gloat but he had to admit he was feeling very pleased with himself. His sister Maria was going to be so pleased!

Before he could bolt into the nearest alleyway a strong hand came down from above hauled him up by the shoulder. That same hand spun him round then cruelly snatched away his prize.

His mouth gaped open in surprise like one of the many fish on the nearby stalls. He had not expected to see Father Carlos Ramirez standing there. Not knowing who he was he froze in fear, terrified that he'd been caught. If they were lucky maybe Maria and Juan could escape.

Yes! That was it! He must be the one to take the blame. It was only right as it had been his idea. While he was thinking it all through the priest slipped a hand inside his robes and withdrew his wallet.

"How much for this melon?" he called out to the distracted seller.

The man dragged his attention away from Juan for a moment.

"Twenty pesos."

"I will take half," said the Father handing him a ten peso note from his wallet.

"Father!" shouted the woman with the injured leg. "This man is possessed! You must help him!"

The crowd murmured their agreement.

Poor Juan faced quite a conundrum now. He had everyone's full attention, but he knew their plan had failed. There was simply no point in continuing the ruse and to be fair the whole thing was quite an exhausting business. But if he just got up and walked away the crowd could quite possibly turn nasty. They were all riled up now and hoping to see an exorcism.

But Father Carlos Ramirez was no fool. He'd grown up on the streets of Bogota and was well acquainted with this sort of scam as well as a few others.

"Here," he said handing the melon to Ricardo. "Take this and go. Be sure to share some of it with your sister."

"Thank you senior," said Ricardo, once he'd got over his shock.

As Father Ramirez walked away the sweet scent of freshly cut melon drifted up into the young boys nostrils. He breathed deeply and shut his eyes as though in a blissful trance.

Thanks to the father they would get to taste watermelon for the very first time. He must remember to thank God also in his prayers tonight.

He took it over to Maria who just stared at it in awe. She had never actually believed that they would succeed. Wonderingly she ran her little birdlike hand over its green rind and cautiously tasted a little drop of the juice that clung to her middle finger. She closed her eyes ecstatically.

"Where is Papa Juan?" she said suddenly.

The sudden pang of shame that surged through him at her question made his cheeks glow. What was he thinking? He should not have left the old man.

"Stay here," he told her, pushing her down behind a pile of cardboard boxes.

Obedient as ever, she nodded and hunkered down at the mouth of the alley way, trembling like a blade of grass in the wind.

Back at the fruit stall Father Ramirez leaned over the stricken man. He shook his head at the drops of sweat that beaded the old man's forehead. He could see he'd exerted himself overmuch. It was time to put this charade to an end.

"I sense no unclean spirit in this man," he declared, laying his hand upon his forehead. "Only a grievous sickness for which there is no cure. He will be with the Lord before long."

At that the crowd backed away a few paces out of fear of contamination. They were wary yet still curious to see how this panned out. When Juan's tired limbs gradually stopped their frantic pedalling people started to move away. They were no longer interested now that there was a simple earthly explanation.

"The coast is clear," whispered the Father conspiratorially. Cautiously Juan opened his eyes, unsure of whether or not to keep up the pretence.

He sat up, then shook his head as though confused.

"There is no need to continue this pretence my friend. I grew up in the slums of Bogota so I know a thing or two about street life," Carlos said with a tired smile.

"Then you will know that I trust no one," answered Juan, struggling to sit up.

"Juan!" cried Ricardo rushing up to them and dropping to his knees. "You are feeling better?"

"Yes, yes," he nodded, patting the boy's shoulder.

"Trust no one eh? I can see that," murmured Carlos drily.

"I should not have left you," the boy said looking remorseful.

"Never mind that. All that matters is that everyone's ok. Where is your sister? Surely you haven't left her alone with that melon? There will be nothing left!"

Juan was quite wrong about that. Maria's attention was not on the melon at all. Although she was surrounded by the hustle and bustle of the busy market place and hidden behind a pile of empty fruit boxes the little girl felt she was on her own. Therefore her senses were understandably heightened to the point where she was poised to flee at the slightest hint of danger.

She sat quietly and waited for her brother to return, her hands gripping either side of their prize. As she shifted position to relieve the ache in her back a noise from behind caught her attention.

Perhaps it was something falling in one of the old abandoned warehouses? The little run down side street she was hiding in was full of them. Her heart thumped wildly as she pondered over what she should do. Perhaps someone was in there? She should move before they came and stole her precious melon.

She took a quick bite out of it in thinking it could be her first as well as her last. There it was again! Something was definitely moving in the building behind her. She could hear it. It sounded like someone creeping around in the darkness. A startled pigeon flew out through the open doorway and almost colliding with her face.

She let out a little shriek. Fear burned bright in the pit of her stomach. She wanted Ricardo! Without even realising what she was doing she took a few steps back until she collided with a figure standing directly behind her.

Heart pounding, she tried to scream, but he clamped a hand tightly around her mouth. Suddenly a cat shot out of the warehouse and disappeared around the corner in belated answer to her earlier curiosity.

"Ever heard the expression, curiosity killed the cat?" the man whispered hotly into her ear.

Maria shook her head violently.

"Well you have now," he said picking her up bodily, melon and all.

He carried her to the end of the street where a rusted up old dumpster was overflowing with rubbish and crawling with rats. Behind it was a car. A police car.

She told herself over and over she must not get in, no matter what. She must not let him take her. Perhaps it was bravery that made her struggle or perhaps it was fear of what might happen should he manage to succeed. Either way something galvanised her into action till she was just a blur of thrashing arms and legs. During the struggle his hand briefly slipped from her mouth giving her the fleeting freedom to release an ear splitting scream.

He cuffed her viciously around the head causing her to drop the melon which exploded with a mushy sound as it hit the pavement. Juice splattered up his neatly pressed trousers mimicking the blood stains from another street child he'd killed only three nights before. Those had taken his wife hours to remove.

Usually their housekeeper took care of such trivial things like the laundry and she was very good at it. But he wasn't entirely sure she could be trusted in matters such as this. Some things required a more personal touch.

If only the girl would stop struggling, he thought. For her size she was quite tenacious.

"Putrid little wretch," he snapped, shaking her furiously.

The girl let out another desperate scream. This time her brother heard and came running.

Not far behind him was Father Ramirez and by his side, Papa Juan who was out of puff and wide eyed like a spectator at the run of the bulls.

"You already rescued one thieving villain today Father," the man called out. "This one's mine!"

"Leave her alone!" shouted Ricardo pelting along the tarmac towards him.

"Ricardo! Papa!" cried Maria reaching out to them in wide eyed desperation.

"Enough!" Fernando Cortez yelled hurling her forcefully into the back of the car.

As it was police car, there was no way to open the door from within. She banged furiously on the blacked out glass, bruising her tiny knuckles. But to no avail. Seeing that Carlos and Juan were almost upon them, Fernando leapt into the driving seat and sped off towards the outskirts of the city.

Maria climbed into the back window of the car and mouthed, "It's ok!"

All Ricardo her brother could do was fall to his knees and yell, "NO!"

Chapter Fifteen

Priorities

"IF I WERE a man I would find her!" cried the boy with the tearstained dirty face. He thumped the steel drum in front of him for emphasis.

"I would ask everyone to help. I would make them listen!" he said almost bursting into tears again.

Juan sighed. Today he felt every single one of his fifty nine years and a lot more. He'd never seen the boy like this before. Not even when he'd hid in the shadows and watched Fernando's men butcher a mindless crack head for talking about things he had no business talking about.

Unable to move he'd sat rooted to the spot till Maria and Juan found him cold and shaking the next morning.

That horrific incident had certainly upset the boy. It would upset most people. The only outward manifestation of that had been the pronounced introversion that had afflicted him for months afterwards. He had been very reluctant to talk. But he had never cried. Not that Juan knew of anyhow.

The two men before him understood why he was so cut up. It was a widely known fact amongst the homeless community that once a child fell into the hands of Fernando Cortez and his men that you might as well wave goodbye to the prospect of ever seeing them again - alive at any rate.

"Listen!" Juan said gently. "The only thing folk like us can count on is each other."

"Well, that and God," he said casting a side long glance at the Father.

The priest looked pensive.

"We will go out, Juan and I. Talk to a few people. See if we can get some support – maybe organise a search party," he said.

Juan gave a soft snort.

"I know you mean well Father, but there's a good chance we may end up disappearing ourselves if we do that. You don't know what it's like at night around here. Why not wait until morning? The three of us can go out and look for her."

"I've got a pretty good idea what it's like. You're forgetting that I was a street child once. Bogota is not much better than here, I can tell you. If we wait until morning we could be too late. We should go now. It still may not do any good. But it is wrong to sit back and do nothing," Carlos said.

"Do not withhold him from doing good, who is able: if thou art able, do good thyself also. Say not to thy friend: Go, and come again: and tomorrow I will give to thee: when thou canst give at present," said Carlos quoting scripture to enhance his argument.

"Please!" Ricardo pleaded, quite literally on bended knee before the two of them.

Juan looked away in frustration biting his lip through his

fuzzy grey beard.

"Ok," he said finally. "You know my concerns. It is not my self I'm worried about. I think there is a strong possibility that four people may wind up dead tonight instead of one. But we will do it. We will go tonight and we will look for Maria. She needs us."

Ricardo closed his eyes and bowed his head.

"Thank you," he whispered.

No one answered – because the others knew he was not addressing anyone in the room.

"May your faith be blessed child," the Father said, wishing with all his heart that it could be so.

Back in the fifth dimension in the realm that lies beyond the reach of practically all mortal life God was working hard to contain a potentially very damaging situation.

Whilst lying on the treatment couch the day before enjoying the skilful hands of his own personal Swedish masseuse, God had seen something unexpected on one of the big screen TVs. At first he just stared at it idly as humans are apt to do when in relaxation mode in the evening. Then the penny dropped that this could be something big. Really BIG. It was something that could affect sentient beings everywhere if it got out of hand – including him. That realisation gave him quite a jolt at first. To say he got into a flap wouldn't be quite right, but it wasn't far off the mark.

He shooed away Henri the masseuse and sat down at his desk to take a closer look.

The aforesaid event was occurring at the CNSA or China National Space Administration where a team of scientists had designed and built a probe and were about to launch it into space.

On its own this was nothing new. God had watched mankind fire their silly insignificant little darts into space many times before and had found it mildly amusing, like a father watching his son pretending to shave in the bathroom mirror.

On this occasion though, it was drastically different. The place they intended to send the probe was a definite no go zone as far as he was concerned. Humans were absolutely not allowed to play with the Ison comet. It was out of bounds end of story.

Yet here were a team of scientist a day and a half away from launching their probe.

Their aim was to identify the composition of the comet and possibly find signs of primitive life if they were extremely lucky. Course that last one would never happen, because God already knew there wasn't any. He'd checked on his last visit to the comet. Their first goal though was eminently achievable if he allowed the launch to go ahead as planned.

As luck would have it, the scientists were Chinese. And God knew that once the Chinese found out what was up there they wouldn't let up until they got their hands on it. Which would in all likelihood lead to a massive power struggle - one that could change the entire balance of power... and not just on Earth.

He needed time to assess the situation and come up with a workable plan of action; one that would keep his secret under wraps and ensure that this situation could never occur again.

Even for the Almighty, that was easier said than done. He sat for hours in his office considering each and every scenario – wondering if there was perhaps something he hadn't thought of. Something that was there right in front of his face, a solution that was mocking him with its sheer simplicity. The natural inclination was to ask for the input of his fellow spirits. But then it wouldn't be his secret any longer, and that was the whole point of the entire exercise – to keep it under wraps, even from them.

When he cancelled not only his daily three o clock massage but also his weekly poker night with Nick everyone in both Heaven and Hell knew that something was seriously off. The last time God had cancelled poker night was in the fourteenth century when the Black Death had swept across Europe killing seventy five million people worldwide – virtually all of them believers. The number of people attending churches and synagogues had taken years to recover. As had happened back then the rumour mill once again went into over drive.

Well, at least it gave them something to think about.

After much thought and careful consideration he finally narrowed his choices down to three options. He could:

Cause the probe to malfunction and hope they wouldn't suspect anything or even worse send another one.

Divert the course of the comet.

Manipulate the results that the probe sent back.

The first option was out for starters because it was pretty much a given that they would simply send another and another if so required until they achieved their aims. The comet Ison had their attention now.

Diverting the course of the comet was his favourite. It seemed to him that if he could just tweak the angle of its trajectory a little he could cause the comet to crash into the heart the sun. Then it would never bother him or humanity again.

The problem was the angle of trajectory was already set. To change it now even in just slightly meant risking discovery. He could just imagine the hoo-ha it would cause if they realised. The conspiracy theorists would go bananas not to mention the scientists. Mankind was nothing if not persistent and extremely imaginative. Give them a mystery to play with and they'd stop at nothing to try and discover what was behind it. Just look at the astonishing lengths people had gone to in order to find out whether or not there really was a Loch Ness Monster. Then there was the subject of aliens. Even governments had funded projects to get to the bottom of that one. The mere whiff of a mystery and all common sense seemed to go out of the window.

No, he decided, that option just risked opening a huge can of worms.

He would have to go with the third option. Manipulating the results would be fairly easy for someone as powerful as him. The chance of discovery was slim, although admittedly it was not impossible given their current state of advancement. There really was no simple solution to this problem. The more they expanded their horizons the harder it was to keep things simple. He felt a bit like earth parents do when trying to keep the truth about Father Christmas from their offspring. He must stall their advancement for as long as possible. They were just not ready yet.

He had to confess he liked the odds. He felt so confident he could make it work he even briefly pondered letting Nick in on the situation to some extent so that they could place bets on the outcome. But that would never do. He might smell a rat and start poking around.

Just then someone interrupted his line of thought with a loud knock on the door. If he'd been thinking straight he'd have recognised the knock as being an urgent one. But as he was just struggling with the Ison dilemma at that particular moment in time he jumped to the conclusion that it was an unwelcome and unnecessary intrusion into his own private space.

What could possibly be more urgent than the current situation? This is what it must feel like when Jehovah's Witnesses knock on the door, he thought to himself. Ever wonder they're so unpopular!

Having ignored the countless view screens that monitored virtually every prominent situation down on earth for the last twenty four hours he'd missed a few important developments. Of course there were safety measures in place should God fail to notice a significant event. One of those safety measures was now at his door bursting to tell him what was happening. Or rather what was going to happen if they didn't stop it.

Bang, bang, bang!

God sighed in vexation.

"Come in!" he said, massaging his temple.

"My Lord," said He'vernon, walking in with her head slightly bowed.

Ingratiatory behaviour such as this had not been uncommon back when she'd been a human. The tribe that she had grown up in was a patriarchal society and He'vernon or He've as she was then known as, had been the only female in the family aside from her mother. Submissiveness and an eagerness to please were second nature to her. So strong were these traits that they carried through into the afterlife. This was, in part why God had thought her a perfect candidate for the job of chief tattletale.

These days it was her job was to watch the other spirits and report any anomalous or potentially harmful behaviour.

"Well? What is it?" said God snappily.

She flinched a little and seemed reluctant to make her report now she was actually before him.

"It's about Sarah," she finally began.

God turned his back to her and rolled his eyes, pretending that he was looking for something in a drawer.

"Right. So what has she done now?" he asked.

He'd taken his tablet from the drawer and was busy updating his MYSPIRIT social media page.

"It never rains but it pours," he wrote.

"Sorry Nick and Gabriel," he wrote tagging them in the post. "Duty calls. Got to cancel blackjack night."

"Well, she hasn't done anything…yet," He'vernon replied. "But you know how I always trust my instincts and my instincts are telling me trouble's brewing again. I'm beginning to think she's a trouble maker."

"Look," said God, setting down the ultrathin tablet. "I know just how badly you want to redeem yourself from messing up last time. So you failed to predict her violent outburst towards Casey. Well at least she didn't kill him. Your reputation will recover."

"You don't understand. This is not about my reputation. It's about Sarah."

"Yes, I know you don't like her," said God.

He'vernon wanted to grind her teeth in annoyance, but she didn't dare. Now that she'd made a mistake and tarnished the record she'd been working so hard to restore she felt she must beyond perfect in order to erase the damage.

She could hardly deny that she disliked Sarah. God would know she was lying. It was probably best if she just move on with her report.

"According to my calculations there is a high probability she may bump into Father Ramirez if she accompanies Casey to Mexico City. You know she had some sort of infatuation for him when they served together at the convent."

"Don't be ridiculous!" he chuckled. "She would hardly know him if she saw him anyway. Last time they had any contact the woman was blind! Look, I really, really don't have time for this right now He've. I have a great many important things to attend to. This universe doesn't run itself you know. As long as she doesn't have another go at bumping Casey off I'll be quite happy. I seriously doubt whether it will ever come up again after the lecture I gave her but if it ever looks like a serious possibility, then don't hesitate to red flag it. For now just put together a report and send it to my in box. I'll take a look later."

She stared at him, dismayed to see that he no longer took her seriously.

"Dismissed," he said, turning his attention back to updating his status.

Feeling stung, she returned to her office cubicle on the top floor of sky scraper number seven and set about writing her report. She just hoped he'd get his act together and read it before it was too late.

Chapter Sixteen

A Return to Flesh

THIS TIME ROUND, Casey had asked to materialise in actual human form. He was desperate to feel the ground beneath his feet again and feel the warmth of the sun on his face.

"If you want me to do this job and do it well, you need to give me some form of respite from my prison cell every once in a while," he had complained to God.

Sarah could not believe he had even asked and was surprised by the response he got. It was not what she had expected at all. She was beginning to think God had a soft spot for Casey.

"Although your crimes were grave, I think you have a point. You may go in human form on this occasion. But I shall be watching closely to see how it turns out," God had said.

He felt especially magnanimous in light of the progress the two of them were making. He hoped soon that they would reach the point where they could operate on their own, with minimal input from him. That's the way he liked things to run so that he could focus on the more important things – things that pertained to his overall purpose.

This unexpected bonus pleased not only Casey but Sarah as well who had not been in physical form for three years.

A short while later they came to, their souls now housed in freshly cloned bodies. Unaccustomed to the light they blinked at the clouds scudding past in the bright blue sky. Movement and speech were not possible until the neurons in their brain had fired a few thousand times. Until then they lay quietly, just enjoying the extraordinary pleasure of being outside, unencumbered by the weight of their limitations as spirits.

Casey was the first to be able to move.

He groaned and rolled over. It felt strange to be able to move again. Probably best take it slow though, he thought sitting up jerkily.

He took in his surroundings then closed his eyes to the gentle sigh of the breeze. He had not known he would feel this way. His senses were in danger of being overloaded unaccustomed as they were to the sensory and emotional input he was now receiving.

Tears leaked from the corners of his eyes making their way to the silky dark strands of his hair. The gift of sight was once again his and the feelings that evoked were overwhelming.

Beside him Sarah was struggling with the same issues. But for her it was slightly different. She had been blind from birth which made the experience all the more profound.

Once she could talk, she gasped at the brightness that surrounded them out in the open. Unable to voice how she felt she choked back the tears - her shoulders shaking and churning up the dust until she actually did begin to choke.

Casey moved closer so that he could help her up, their

shared vulnerability uniting them.

"It's a weird feeling isn't it?" he said, brushing the dust from her hair.

She nodded and clung to his waist. There was nothing to say because their growing connection said it for them. He looked down at her in wonderment. No one had ever held him like this before and the fact that she could when she knew what he'd done made it all the more touching. Sarah was one surprising woman.

The two of them sat like that for a few moments drawing comfort from each other's presence until the silence was suddenly shattered by a series of explosive gunshots. They both jumped in surprise. A couple of jet black crows flew off, startled - protesting indignantly at the unwelcome disturbance.

"That sounded close," said Casey looking uneasy. "What happens if we get hurt or killed whilst in these bodies? *Can we get hurt or killed?*"

"I don't know. It's probably something we should have asked."

"You should have asked you mean," Casey replied.

She ignored him her eyes now trained on a series of tumble down shacks about a quarter of a mile away.

"I think it came from over there," she said.

"Do you think it's our man Fernando up to no good?"
She shrugged.

"Don't know. It would seem likely. God has obviously put us here for a reason."

"You think so? You're still holding onto the hope there is a rational, benevolent motive behind everything that God does then?" She stood up and brushed herself off, ignoring the loaded question.

"Come on," she commanded. "We've got work to do."

She set off in the direction of the derelict buildings clearly expecting him to follow. Casey felt an unexpected twinge of disappointment. He'd been enjoying that moment of connection that they had shared as brief as it was. Such things were rare in his life. Pity that he'd ruined it with his sarcastic comment.

His lesson learnt he followed her closely wondering what they were going to find.

The two of them covered the distance to the shacks quickly in the hope that they could catch Fernando before he left. Outside they encountered a police car from the Xochimilco district. It was dusty and splattered with dead flies.

It didn't take long for them to guess that probably it belonged to Fernando, the guy they were after. The file had said he was the Chief of police in the Xochimilco district. It had also said he was a very dangerous man.

This as well as the fact that they were now in human bodies made them both very cautious. A noise from the direction of the buildings caused them to duck for cover. Hunkering down by the passenger side door they breathed heavily, wondering what to do.

"This is crazy," she whispered, brushing her hair from her eyes.

Casey waited for her to elaborate.

"What?" he said.

"Us being here with this homicidal cop. He kills children for heavens' sake! There's no way he's going to think twice before killing us. I've died once already. I have no wish to die again thank you very much. I think we should go and check with God before we go any further," whispered Sarah excitedly.

"It's a bit late for that! Shhh…I think someone's coming…"

Casey ducked down again. He'd been peeping through the passenger side door. Through the open window they heard the police radio spring into life all static and crackle.

"All cars. All units."

A buzz of static resumed for a few seconds then the voice returned.

"All cars, all units. Officer Cortez has been abducted. The prime suspect is a man named Father Carlos Ramirez. You have orders to shoot on sight if he attempts to avoid arrest. Repeat, shoot on sight. Father Ramirez is also wanted in connection with the murder of a young child named Maria we just discovered on the outskirts of the city along with her brother Ricardo and an old man who as of yet remains unidentified. The global positioning unit inside Fernando's car puts it at these co-ordinates. Nineteen point one three zero zero degrees north by ninety nine point four zero zero zero degrees west. Unit seven and twelve please proceed to these co-ordinates to investigate further. Be sure to exercise extreme caution as the suspect is armed and remember that the safety of the Chief is paramount. Over."

Sarah and Casey looked at each other in alarm. What was going on? Surely it was Fernando who was the killer.

"This is unit seven reporting. On our way to the scene right now. We should be there within the next ten minutes. Over."

"Copy that. Keep us informed as to the situation. Over."

"Affirmative," came the reply.

The crunch of footsteps coming towards them grabbed their attention. What were they going to do? And more to the point who was it?

A car door opened and someone sat down heavily causing the car to tilt on one side. Before either of them could do anything the occupant had turned the key in the ignition and started to pull away at break neck speed. Through the cloud of orange dust that enveloped the car they were able to make out that the driver was indeed Carlos.

Sarah stood watching the car speed away in disbelief. What had he done? And why was he stealing the car? A little voice in the back of her mind offered up an answer but she didn't want to believe it.

"Over here!" shouted Casey. He stood in the door way of the nearest shed beckoning her to him. Sarah's feet were glued to the ground. She didn't want to see.

"What is it?" she said.

"See for yourself."

Steeling herself she joined him to see what he had found. Her worst fears were confirmed.

"Looks as though someone beat us to it. I'm going to take a wild guess here and say it was your friend Carlos. He did the job for us," he said, staring down at the body of Fernando. A single bullet to the head had extinguished the corrupt police officers life for good.

"No. No! He would never do that," insisted Sarah. "He's a good man. He's not capable of such things. You don't know him like I do."

She stopped, realising she was starting to babble.

"Maybe...but people change. You know they do."

Disgusted by the stench of death and its implication Sarah

fled from the shed and vomited outside behind an empty chicken coup. Struggling for breath she leaned up against the wall.

"I guess having a physical body isn't all it's cracked up to be," said Casey appearing beside her. He smiled sympathetically, unsure of what to say.

"You knew him well, this Carlos guy?" he said trying again.

She opened her mouth as if about to say something but then closed it again at the sound of approaching sirens.

"We should go," said Casey emphatically.

"I don't know what's happened. But I'm not leaving him to cope with the fall out of this on his own. He needs my help," she croaked.

"Don't be stupid. A few minutes ago you were scared stiff of putting yourself in any physical danger and now you're talking about helping a fugitive who has no idea you even exist. You do the math Sarah! How is that going to work exactly?"

"I don't know. But I do know something has happened to him. Carlos needs my help. They will kill him if they find him," she said flatly. "He deserves better."

"If this means so much to you, why not ask God for help? You're still a believer aren't you? One of the good guys? And you have the added advantage of being able to stand before him in his literal presence and ask him for help. People on earth don't have that privilege."

Sarah knew he was right. She also knew this was a test. Firstly he was trying to test the level of her faith. But behind it she also knew he had selfish motivations – namely self-preservation and she could hardly blame him for that. She herself had been afflicted by it earlier. If Casey died whilst acting as Karma and housed in a physical body there was every chance that that would be it for him. He'd most likely wind up in Hell. His reasoning was sound.

But was hers?

Before her death she had been an ardent believer and she still was. But if she was honest with herself her faith had undergone a transformation of sorts once faced with the reality of Heaven and the Supreme Being himself.

Previously she had been in denial over this but now she was required to gambol the life of the man she loved on her faith in the divine she was having considerable difficulty. But there was more to this situation than met the eye. She had watched the man in front of her make radical changes to his thinking and behaviour and not just in the name of God. He was showing evidence of wanting to be a better person, of seeing the difference between right and wrong and had displayed what could only be described as compassion on more than one occasion.

For her to display a lack of faith at a time like this could kill off whatever seeds of spirituality that were germinating in his heart. His progress had been slow and painful. It had been three years since his attack on Valentina. Back then the task of making that self- serving piece of human detritus a useful member of society had seemed impossible. But with persistence and a little help from God she'd made a surprising amount of head way.

The approaching sirens sealed the deal. As hard as it was she knew what she had to do.

"Come," she said simply. Taking his hand she turned inwards and stepped into the spirit realm. Her metaphysical heart thumped at the gravity of what she had done. She could almost picture Carlos's dead body lying in a ditch as she climbed the first step on the stairway to heaven. In her mind she could see him lying on his back, mutilated and stripped naked – because that's what those kind of people would do. Casey watched her in silence knowing that she was being tortured with thoughts of what if.

"We've got to make him listen."

Although he had his doubts, Casey nodded in agreement. As they reached the top of the stair way he reached across and took her hand, hoping to make up for his past misdeeds. His action comforted her and gave her the confidence that she was about to do what was right.

Chapter Seventeen

Minion

THE DEVIL SURVEYED his kingdom and almost wept with happiness. It was the same pretty much every time he did so – such was his satisfaction in all he had wrought.

Suffering was his business. Pain was his chosen art form. There was nothing he wouldn't consider in order to inflict pain upon his subjects.

There were endless psychological torments, torments that were designed to stretch the subject's normal pain threshold to its very limit, impending doom scenarios, hallucination chambers where the individual experienced every form of death imaginable and much, much, more.

His favourite were the psychological trials he put the sinners through. Such as the endless queues for water, a highly sort after commodity in a place as hot as Hell. The queues went on and on for miles but when they eventually got there the water had run out or else evaporated.

Another method was the falling lift scenario, where the

person got into an elevator having been told their being in Hell was all a big mistake. They were then told that the lift would take them back to Earth. The lift then climbed steadily upwards then dropped like the proverbial stone, hitting the ground with bone shattering impact. As soon as the subject recovered himself it climbed steadily upwards before repeating the whole sequence all over again.

He derived much joy from that one. It was one of his favourites. His was the type of character that revelled in the perverse. Like a little boy who took pleasure in pulling wings off insects only to an incredibly magnified degree.

As much he enjoyed it he sometimes grew weary of the same old same old just like anyone else. Sometimes he felt the need to stretch his wings a little so to speak; to look beyond the lakes of fire and sulphur and the dissection laboratories and experience something different. That was why, trivial as it was, he looked forward to the evenings he spent with God and Gabriel playing blackjack, poker and the listening to the occasional cabaret performance.

"What do you think he's up to?" he said scratching one of his demonic minions under the chin as though he was a dog.

The scaly red creature hissed and fawned upon his hand affectionately.

"I do not know my Lord," it said flicking its tail. "But if it pleases you I can investigate?"

"Your loyalty will be rewarded," smiled Satan patting his head. "It is not a big issue however. I am merely curious as to why God has cancelled the cosy little diversion we had scheduled for this evening. Be sure to be discreet. The others need not know."

The demon bowed his head and raised himself up from the

foot of the golden throne.

"I will endeavour to please you with total obedience," declared the spirit. "And nothing less than perfection in this matter."

"You serve me well Isakar. Report back to me with your findings."

"Yes my Liege."

Satan watched as he flew away until he became a small dot of black on the shimmering horizon leaving him alone with his thoughts.

What could possibly be going on that required poker night and blackjack night to be cancelled? Perhaps it was something with Casey again?

He doubted it. Maybe it was something entirely new. He sure hoped so. He could do with something interesting to spice up his week. He tapped his long nails on the arm of the throne and turned things over in his mind for a little while.

He found not knowing what was going on annoying. *What could it possibly be?*

Ever since that scandal about paedophile priests in the Catholic Church God had been a lot more reluctant to keep him in the loop. Perhaps that was it. Perhaps that's what this was all about.

Once his interest was piqued, there was no way he could sit back and wait until Isakar came back with news. For all he knew he might not even have any!

No. He would take things into his own hands and pay God an unannounced visit. That would surely shake things up.

He swooped into God's shamefully luxurious office as silent as death. But he was wasting his time. God had heard him and he was as mad as a hatter at the intrusion.

"What are you doing here?" he snarled. He was so harsh and threatening it terrified even the Devil.

Recoiling, Satan took a step back and fell across the desk which subsequently broke in half and turned into a puff of smoke dropping him to the floor.

God's secretary buzzed through from the other side of the door, worried about the commotion.

"Everything alright my Lord?" she asked pleasantly.

"Yes, Martha. Continue with your duties," he said sharply.

"Of course," she responded lightly.

"You know there *are* rules Be-Beelzebub," God warned him. "You are never supposed to come here uninvited."

Energy crackled between the two, sparking like Saint Elmo's fire. Satan looked as though he was going to protest but instead he threw his hands up in the air.

"I know! I know! I shouldn't have," he admitted. "But when you cancelled blackjack night and poker night it got me pretty worried. So I decided to come up here and see what was going on. You'd have done the same. I always make a point of studying my opponent. I know you well, whether you like it or not."

"So you're telling me you're here out of concern?" said God mocking him cruelly. "Awww…I think I've come over all warm and fuzzy."

"What do you take me for knuckle head!" he sneered giving him a back hander across the face.

The Devil just laughed and licked the blood tenderly from his lips.

"You're pretty het up considering nothing's going on," he

commented slyly.

"There's always something going on with these humans. You know that," God told him, trying to dissemble.

"Ok, have it your way," said the Devil suddenly. "I just thought that you valued my input. We've worked well together on things in the past."

"This is not a partnership. There is a hierarchy and I'm at the top of the food chain. You'd do well to remember that if ever you feel the urge to burst in uninvited again."

The Devil stared at him blankly, trying to get a feel for what was behind all this cloak and dagger. He had known that God wouldn't be too impressed with him just dropping in, but his reaction seemed rather disproportionate to his actions.

Could it be that he felt threatened in some way? That this overreaction to his unexpected presence was the equivalent of a male silver back beating his chest in the rain forest? He had said something about hierarchy and him being the man at the top.

The Devil got up and slunk away from his office deep in thought. Not much point in staying when he was clearly getting nowhere.

He'd just have to wait for Isakar to report back to him but in the mean time he'd amuse himself by stirring up a little trouble down in Mexico City. Sister Sarah could do with a little fun in her boring hum drum existence.

Chapter Eighteen

Chain of Command

"HOW MANY DAYS away from earth is the comet now?" Han'mei's superior asked. He was leaning over her shoulder in that way that always maddened her. His sweet and sour noodle breath was wafting over her shoulders in a way that set her teeth on edge.

"Fourteen point seven," she said pointing to the count down at the bottom of her screen. Her fingers flew over the keyboard as she performed her hourly check on the probes condition.

"We should be getting data from the probe within the next eight hours or so then," he said. "It's been there long enough to have gathered sufficient samples from the surface. Be sure to inform me the moment you get the results."

"Of course, Mr Chang."

It seemed as though the conversation had come to a natural conclusion but he continued to hang around. Han'mei found this unnerving. She wished he would say what he had to say and leave.

"By now the American's must know we have sent it," he said eventually. "They will be sure to try to intercept the package or possibly send their own probe."

Han'mei supressed a grimace and nodded. She hated his paranoia and the way he ran constant espionage checks on her and the rest of the staff. Rather than encourage their loyalty it damaged team morale. They were always suspicious or under suspicion.

She failed to see why it was necessary. It was just a hunk of burning rock and gas, only of interest to scientists and astronomers. Although she would never say so she saw nothing wrong with sharing the information they found with the global scientific community anyway. They were all on the same side – the side of humanity.

Sad to say, experience had taught her that taking such action would be extremely unwise. If discovered she would be executed. She didn't just work for CNSA. She was an employee of the Chinese Government. And they took loyalty very seriously. Deadly serious.

So she kept her thoughts to herself and concentrated fiercely on the screen in front of her. She smiled when Mr Chang eventually got bored of hovering in the back ground and moved off to harass someone else. Concentrating so hard left her with a sore neck so she got up and went over to the cafeteria for a coffee in the hope that it would wake her up a little.

The coffee cup felt comfortingly warm between the palms of her hands in stark contrast to the bitterly cold weather conditions outside. Through the window she could see that snow was falling steadily, piling up on the hoods of the cars parked in front of the building. Drifts were forming against every available edifice, blocking the doors and fire exits. A team of workmen had just arrived to clear the way.

It was tempting to stay and enjoy the scene but her phone beeped loudly, letting her know that the results had started to come in from the probe.

Reluctantly she picked up her coffee and made her way back to the laboratory.

"Mr Chang!" she exclaimed, in surprise upon finding him leaning over her desk. "Did you lose something?"

His hands seemed to searching for something but she had no idea what. Her sudden return had clearly startled him. He quickly covered it over by wielding his authority.

"Where have you been Han'mei?" he scolded. "You were needed here to decipher the code."

Suddenly the screen resolution increased.

"That's better," he said straightening up. "It's a wonder you can work at all in this half-darkness."

He moved aside so that she could sit down. Why did he have to be so controlling? She'd already told him she would call him the moment results were in. His constant hovering around was unnerving.

She opened up the program she'd designed to decipher the encryption code and leaned back in her chair. It creaked like her grandmothers bones beneath her weight.

"This could take a while," she said hoping he would go away.

"That's alright, it will give us time to talk," he said. She didn't like the sound of that.

Three hours later on the other side of the world the closest thing to her counterpart opened up an email he'd been expecting.

"Damn," Austin muttered under his breath. It was not what

he had hoped.

According to the anonymous email the Chinese had discovered that the comet was mainly composed of rock, gases, methanol, ethanol, hydrogen cyanide and formaldehyde. The only surprise in there was the small traces of gold and platinum.

Once his initial disappointment had passed he reminded himself that it was no bad thing really because if the Chinese had found anything of value either on the scientific front or from a resources point of view it would have caused a pretty big stink within his department and who knew what other ramifications.

Opinion within the department had been divided on whether or not to send up their own probe. The final decision had been made by Austin. It was a tough call. But his greatly diminished budget swung the final vote.

As the weeks and months went by, though, he had begun to wonder if he'd made the right decision. Perhaps he should have let himself be guided by his gut instinct instead of the all-important dollar sign. Supposing the Chinese made a ground breaking discovery up there? They would never know unless the Chinese Government decided to share that knowledge.

This second guessing himself had continued for many weeks until he received an unexpected email just as he was shutting down his laptop for the night.

The email was from someone purporting to be an employee of the CNSA. Initially Austin had doubts about the validity of such claims but upon questioning the individual via series of emails he discovered that this was in fact the truth.

The individual wanted US citizenship in exchange for sensitive information – namely the result of the probes findings.

Austin was not sure they could offer that but he strung them along for a while anyway. Eventually the identity of the potential defector was revealed, who turned out to be none other than the director of astrophysics at the CNSA – Mr Xi Chang. That was when it turned deadly serious so he had brought their *own* director in on it who sought presidential approval enabling the three of them to strike a deal.

For a long time everything went quiet leading Austin to wonder whether he had perhaps been found out and executed. That was until the email he'd just received.

He watched the live feed of Ison blazing across the sky, zooming in to see the coma, a tenuous atmosphere created by dust and gas that the comet released.

Suddenly the comet turned a violent orange colour with a lurid purple edge and a shock wave sped outwards from it like a psychedelic tsunami. Austin almost fell off his chair. As he watched in fascination his hand snaked out to grab the phone.

"Martin, are you seeing this?" he said in childlike wonder.

"Seeing what?" asked the director. It must have been his lunch break because he could hear him chewing on a bagel or something.

"Switch to Ison's main feed. Hurry," he said urgently.

Martin, the director, did as he was told.

"What the heck?" he said scratching his head. "What's happening?"

"I have no idea."

"Looks like some sort of explosion."

Austin agreed.

"Have we any idea what could have caused it?"

Austin shrugged forgetting that the other man couldn't see him.

"Get onto our man Mr Chang. We need some answers," Martin ordered.

"Yes, Sir. Right away."

Chapter Nineteen

Carlos Who?

"WHO IS IT now?" snapped God when Martha his receptionist buzzed him again.

"It's Karma and Sarah. Shall I send them through?"

He rolled his eyes in annoyance. He needed time to think and so far all he'd gotten were interruptions.

"Is it important?" he said.

There was a brief pause while she quizzed them as to the nature of their visit.

"Apparently so, my Lord."

"Ok. Send them in," he said stifling a sigh.

The double doors to his office opened and in walked the hot nun and her underworld sidekick. What could they possibly want, he wondered? Their task had been a simple one had it not?

"Well?" he said forming a steeple with his fingers. Sarah stared at them, her mind a long way off from where it should be.

Casey cleared his throat and brought her back to reality.

"How did it go?" God repeated. He looked impatient, which

was never a good way to start a conversation with him.

"The objective was achieved," she said, drawing herself up to her full height.

"But…? I get the feeling there's a but in there somewhere," God replied gazing at her in a very intimidating way. The unusual way she had phrased it had grabbed his attention.

It was difficult for Sarah to know how to answer. She did not want to incriminate Carlos or make it sound as though they had been derelict in their duty. Casey seeing her dilemma took over the conversation.

"Someone kind of beat us to it. When we got there we found Fernando already dead. Single tap wound to the head," he explained.

God did not look too surprised. He had been around for a long time and had seen a good many things.

"How very helpful of them. Do you know who this person is?" he asked, standing up to pace around his desk. He fiddled with a paper weight whilst waiting for an answer.

"I think so."

"Who?"

Sarah and Casey looked at each other briefly, united by fear and what they had been through. It was not supposed to be this way. Casey seeing her apprehension was greater than his spoke for them.

"It was Carlos Ramirez."

"The Priest?" said God, looking directly at Sarah.

"Yes." She cast her eyes downwards and for a moment or two there was silence as God appeared to be thinking this through.

"Perhaps I'm missing something here…but I'm stumped as

to how this is supposed to be important to me," he said eventually.

Before either of them could answer something on one of the big screen TVs caught his eye and he snatched up the remote as though to turn up the volume.

Casey felt a wave of relief wash over him. Thank God for that! He wasn't angry about someone else doing the job for them and no one was going to be punished. He couldn't quite believe it. The God he knew from the occasional sermon he had heard in school had always seemed very ready to punish and discipline.

"So you're not mad then?" he asked.

"Why would I be mad?" said God raising a quizzical eyebrow.

Casey shrugged.

"As long as the job's done why worry?" God said. "A wealth of experience as well as numerous complicated mathematical algorithms carried out by my staff told me that Fernando needed to be made an example of. His actions have affected far too many people. He is now undergoing formal processing to see if he meets the entry criterion for Hell. I think we all know how that will go. So what on earth would I be unhappy about?"

He looked at their faces and saw the conflict within.

"Or... perhaps the question should be - what are you two unhappy about?"

Something within Sarah blossomed with gratitude that he had recognised her plight. This was the God she recognised from the old testament – the one that had heard the prayers of the prophet Samuels mother, Hannah, when her childless state had become too much to bear. The weathered edifice of Sarah's faith was bolstered a little – enough at least to tell her Lord what was troubling her.

"We are concerned about Father Ramirez," she said. "He is a wanted man now. The authorities will not let him get away without a fight."

"What Sarah is saying," interrupted Casey. "Is that we're more than happy to go back down there and sort this out for you."

"There is nothing to sort out," God said flatly. "The situation has been contained. Now there are other matters that require my attention."

Still Sarah clung to hope like a survivor clings to a lifebuoy.

"Yes, but they will most likely kill him. Carlos has nowhere to hide and nowhere to go. He is a good man. You know that! We cannot let him die!"

"Do not presume to tell me what I can and cannot do!" God said in a stentorian voice. The force of his ire was enough to knock them off their feet.

Not daring to look up Sarah stayed where she was face down on the ground, trembling like a leaf. Casey laid his hand over hers reassuring her that he was still there. His touch was one of infinite kindness. The strength of it brought tears to her eyes.

"I see that you have learnt gratitude," God said noticing this unusual gesture of tenderness.

Casey did not trust himself to speak. Before him was a being who expected love, devotion, compassion, empathy, trust, selflessness, kindness and many other things from his devotee's. Yet he had seen little in the way of that at first hand from him. Yes the bible and other religious works spouted countless instances of such events yet the most notable ones had all happened in the past.

Why was that?

"Sarah has trained you well. And you should indeed be grateful to her. The time for that is now at an end though. She will accompany you no longer."

Sarah looked up at this unexpected announcement.

"But before you are given full title of Karma along with all the powers that that entails you must fulfil one last mission."

"Which is…?"

"Which is a relatively simple one. You must find someone deserving of good Karma; someone who has filled their life with selfless deeds or who has done one specific thing of extraordinary worth. When you return I expect a full report on all the whys and wherefores. Please close the door on your way out."

He turned away, his interest already on something new. He cranked up the volume on one of the TVs and plumped himself down to watch.

The house where Fernando's car was parked appeared deserted save for a mangy looking cat grooming itself on the veranda. It was a grand sort of place for the likes of Mexico City. Painted and landscaped with tall neatly trimmed hedges of Mexican orange blossom separating it from its nearest neighbour.

"I thought you said he would be here?" complained Casey kicking the cat off the top step.

"Don't kick the cat!" said Sarah.

"Why not? Karma for all those mice he eats," laughed Casey.

"So where is he?"

"I don't know," Sarah admitted. "He should be here. The

car's here."

"Well, if he's this good at hiding perhaps he isn't in as much trouble as we thought."

"You know that's not true. They will find him in the end. And when they do it will not end well for Carlos."

"Well if we can't find him how are the cops going to track him down?"

"They've got more informers than a zebras got stripes Casey. You should know that."

He shrugged and narrowed his eyes at the sun, "I guess the life that taught me those kind of things seems a long way off now. Perhaps it wasn't even my life at all."

"Look," she said. "I can do this on my own from here. You don't need me messing things up for you. For once in your life things are finally going in the right direction and I don't want to get in the way. You're one step away from being made Karma – a privilege that carries a lot of weight and responsibility not to mention privileges. You start getting mixed up with a renegade ex-nun that's gone off the rails and all that will go up in smoke."

"So you're the bad influence now?" Casey said with a grin. "I like it."

She gave him a wry smile – half annoyed half amused.

"I mean it. We should part company."

"And what if I don't want to?"

She sighed and looked heavenward in frustration.

"You are so stubborn!" she said with a shake of her head.

As they had returned to their human bodies Casey took the opportunity to dig her in the side with his elbow.

"And you're not, I suppose?"

"No I'm not," she said folding her arms.

"Suit yourself," he said walking on without her.

"Hey! Where are you going?"

"I want to wash off this dust and sweat. I smell like rhinos butt crack."

"And just where do you propose we do that? And what makes you even think we have the time to do that?"

"We should make the time. We'll be able to think much clearer afterwards. I bet the guy who lives here has a spa or a swimming pool somewhere. Probably out back," Casey speculated. "Come on! It won't take a minute."

His guess was right on the money. In fact he also had an outside shower and there were several large bath towels drying on the washing line.

"Thank you God!" said Casey looking heavenward and pressing his palms together.

Sarah gave him the oddest of looks. But he couldn't be bothered to decipher it.

Quickly the two of them undressed and whilst Casey swam about in the free form swimming pool Sarah freshened up in the outdoor shower enclosure.

"This feels sooo…good!" Sarah heard him say.

"Better than getting stoned?" she called out.

"That's a completely different kind of good," he answered. With a flick of his arms and legs he'd turned over and swam at a leisurely pace on his back.

"Well just remember, we don't have long," she told him. "Fernando's colleagues could arrive here at any moment in search of Carlos. The car has a built in tracking device. And the longer we leave it till we start tracking him the further he'll be away from us."

"I know," he said climbing out of the pool.

She smiled at his readiness to help her although he had obviously been enjoying himself. She too understood his appreciation of this simple pleasure. For someone who'd just come from heaven it was heaven being able to feel the sun on her face again whilst the water cascaded over her body. She loathe to admit it but she also was enjoying being back on earth. But that's the way it was reputed to be with guilty pleasures and things that you just couldn't have.

Meanwhile something had caught Casey's eye whilst swimming, something that warranted a closer look.

"Where are you going?"

"I'm just going over there to check something out," he called over his shoulder.

She peeped through the plastic saloon style shower doors. "What's he up to now?" she muttered.

She stepped out of the shower and squeezed the excess water from her hair. Quickly she dressed and followed him to the strip of waste ground just behind the house.

As with many parts of Mexico affluence and dilapidation co-exist side by side. The waste ground had afforded makeshift housing for someone at one time or another – perhaps gardeners or servants at the house. Crates had been nailed together to make a rough sort of lean to and further afield a rickety looking shed housed a homebrewed moonshine distillery. Creaking in the wind the whole thing had a barely discernible sway as though it had been drinking the very stuff it was built to conceal.

"Someone's in there," whispered Sarah.

Casey put his finger to his lips indicating that she should stay quiet. She nodded and fell in behind him. He crept forward carefully, doing his best to avoid the tin cans and broken car parts strewn here and there over the ground. When he reached the door he stopped. He had heard what sounded like a gun being cocked. Hesitation held him in its powerful grasp.

The sound of desperately heavy breaths dragged him loose. Someone was about to pull the trigger. Someone was about to die. Yanking open the door he rushed inside to find Carlos crouched on the floor with a gun jammed towards the roof of his mouth. His eyes were squeezed shut as he prepared to end it all.

"Carlos, no!"

He turned at the sound of Sarah's voice, his mouth losing its grip on the gun. It fell to the floor as he jumped up, pressing himself against the back wall. His shock at seeing her robbed him of the power of speech. It would be some time till he found the strength to speak again.

Fifteen minutes later he lay in the back of the car that Casey had boosted closing his eyes, full of emotional pain, confusion and far too many regrets. What was Sarah doing here? Was it even her? Just how far gone was he? No. NO. He couldn't think about that now. It was overwhelming. He ignored the cars other two occupants and stared up through the sun roof. Too long he'd struggled against the degradation of his faith and it had worn him down till there was almost nothing left.

It was time he faced the truth. There was no God – at least none that he could discern at work in the world.

How many times had he seen people broken and distraught,

murdered and lost? Too many to number.

And what was it all for? Much of what he had seen in his life made no sense at all. There had been no rhyme or reason to Sarah's death and no one could explain it without evoking the age old mantra of Catholicism – "it's God's will."

If any human being here on earth displayed the desire to take another's life for their own ends they were labelled as having homicidal tendencies. So why was this an acceptable quality in the Supreme Being? Rather than believe there was a creator who sat back and let his children maim and kill each other for countless centuries and snuffed out their lives whenever it suited his purpose, Carlos had reached the point where he'd rather not believe.

This realisation was what had led him to the decision to kill Fernando. When he had seen what he had done to little guileless Maria who had never done anybody any harm he no longer felt he could take the position of benevolent bystander. If he did so he would be no better than the God he had rejected.

Within his power was the capability to ensure that no one ever suffered at Fernando's hands again. It was too good any opportunity to pass up. Any previous reasoning that may have held him back disappeared when he looked down at poor Maria's tiny abused body.

He would not allow him to do this again! If God would not stop him then he would take matters into his own hands. If he had to answer to the authorities for his actions then so be it. They were probably as corrupt as Fernando in any case, if not more so.

His thoughts carried him on a lazy tide. It had no direction – or so it seemed. As the car bumped along and the shadows lengthened his head began to loll and sleep eventually found him.

When he awoke there was no longer any sign of the car or it's other two occupants. He was alone, lying out in the open resting on a heap of refuse piled up behind a building. There were no lights; only the moon and stars. Perhaps they had abandoned him. Or perhaps they'd never even been there in the first place.

A sigh left his body, both deep and lengthy as he searched the heavens above. Still his frustrations remained. Who knew what lay out there, in the big blue sky, beyond the darkness and the glittering expanse of stars? Whatever it was, his considerable intellect could no longer entertain the concept of an 'Almighty God'.

The bitterness of it all choked him with its fury. It was all he'd ever known - like the air inside his lungs and the earth beneath his feet. He hung his head and tried to steady himself.

But he could find no centre of calm. It was lost – there was none.

His thoughts were muddled – full of questions that had no discernible answers. After travelling the globe and studying almost everything he'd ever come across, he recognised that the whole 'God' concept was not what mankind imagined it to be at all and that for the time being at least we are all very, very much alone. We are all street children, he told himself.

The twisting melee of his thoughts was suddenly interrupted by the sound of a bird squawking. Most likely it was a chicken he thought listening to its outraged clucking.

Without warning it burst around the corner of the filling station, half flapping its wings half trotting as though being chased by the Devil himself. Carlos raised himself up on his elbows to get a better look – straining his eyes in the moonlight. Seconds later a woman followed brandishing a stick in club like fashion against her shoulder. From the other direction a man appeared, facing the chicken head on. The unfortunate fowl did not stand much of a chance and was taken out by two well aimed blows to the head.

With her back still facing Carlos, the woman bent down and scooped up the chicken, holding it by its feet.

"Happy now?" she said to the man.

"I'll be a lot happier once it's cooked," he replied.

"You expect me to cook as well?" the woman complained.

"Well, I certainly can't. But I can light a fire," he said going off to find some combustibles.

"You're such a cave man," she scolded, turning towards Father Ramirez.

He looked terrified. Closing his eyes he sat crossing himself repeatedly then after a few moments he slowly opened his eyes as though hoping against hope that the strange apparition had gone away.

"Ahhh!" he cried upon discovering Sarah sitting at his elbow. Panic engulfed him and sent icicles stabbing through his veins.

"Don't be afraid," said Sarah, looking concerned. She had no idea her presence would have such an effect on him. She wanted to reach out and touch him – to reassure him, but she was scared that may push him over the edge.

It was fortunate that she didn't. Her voice alone was quite enough for him to deal with. She sounded just like the Sarah that he used to know and love. But he knew it could not be, for he had found her body lying smouldering in the field several years ago. He had helped lower her coffin into the ground.

"How can this be?" he stammered backing away from her.

"Shh...do not concern yourself Father," she said throwing caution to the wind and kindly taking him by the hand.

"Do not touch me!" he cried, shaking her hand off.

The irony of his actions was not lost on him. Whilst she had been alive he would have done almost anything to be the recipient of such a gesture.

Realising that she had gone very quiet he looked up and found her praying silently.

This surprised him. As far as he knew ghosts do not pray. He watched her closely, needing no further reassurance that it really was her. She was just the way he remembered her – apart from the clothes and the fact that she could now see. She was beautiful, almost angelic.

That thought stopped him in his tracks. *Could it be that that's what she was – an angel?*

"Who are you?" he asked when she had finally stopped praying.

She gave him a look of mild reproof.

"Carlos. You know who I am. But whether or not you choose to believe it is another matter."

Casey approached them with a pile of fire wood.

"Slacking I see. Haven't you plucked and prepared that chicken yet?" he said throwing down the wood crossly.

"This is Father Carlos Ramirez," Sarah told him. "Carlos, this is Casey Davenport." She hoped making a formal introduction might ease the tension a little. It seemed best not to push him. He had been through a lot by looks of things. She lifted the lifeless bird onto her lap and started plucking away the dirty white feathers.

Casey had never shook hands with anyone in his life. But he was willing to make an exception in this instance. He wiped his mucky hands on his trousers and extended his hand in greeting.

"Hi!" he said.

Carlos stared at it for a second then shook it limply. Now that he was closer, Casey could see his features a little better. He took note of the strained expression on his pallid features and took a wild guess that he must have known Sarah quite well before she died. Seeing her again had shook him up pretty good by the looks of things, as it would anyone.

"What are you doing here Sarah?" he murmured.

Seeing that the two of them needed some privacy, Casey moved away to find a suitable spot for the fire. Away from the building would be best. But it still needed to be somewhere that would hide the smoke that would ascend from the fire.

He decided upon a sheltered area in the lea of a pile of boulders that had been dumped in a corner – most likely from when the gas station had first been built. Ignoring the intense exchange going on behind him he set about his task with a rumbling empty stomach.

Chapter Twenty

Contingency Plan

MR CHANG LOOKED around the dull, featureless room eyeing everyone on Project Ison severely.

"Well?" he barked. "Anyone care to explain to me what just happened?"

A painful silence ensued. This could get serious. Mr Chang could either be on a fault finding mission or a fact finding mission. The next few moments would no doubt tell which one it was to be. No one dared to say anything. Most of them could scarcely breathe. All except for Han'mei.

Her mind was racing as she struggled to formulate the answers that Mr Chang required. She loved puzzles especially if they were of a scientific nature.

She raised her Ipad into the air and waited for his permission to speak. He nodded and she began to explain her theory as best she could.

"We all agree that what we just saw was a very unusual event. Explosions are virtually unheard of on comets, although there have been a few, the most recent example being the comet Elenin. But the explosion we just witnessed on Ison appeared to be very different in nature to the one just mentioned. The diffuse shock wave that spread outwards from the blast was highly unusual in appearance and colouration. However it is the strange mixture of both orange and purple that is the clue we need when it comes to identifying the cause."

She pulled up a picture on her iPad and handed it to the person next to her who in turn passed it to the next and so on.

"What you can see here and what we just witnessed on the comet Ison are one and the same. Both are explosions triggered by the presence of the rare earth element Trivarium and the much more common element Titanium."

There was a hush in the room as what she said sunk in.

"Yes but the probe never revealed the presence of Trivarium," said Mr Chang carefully.

"Neither did it reveal the presence of Titanium, but we know it was there."

"How can you say that?" said another member of their group. His name was Richard.

"Because the probe itself was made of Titanium," murmured Mr Chang staring at Han'mei.

"Are you saying the data that the probe sent back was inaccurate? How could that be?" Richard protested.

No one seemed to know.

"It all points to a traitor in our midst," concluded Chang gravely.

Just then a call came through his ear piece informing him that Government officials were on their way to debrief every person present at the facility.

His orders were to perform a full security lock down.

"Right away," he said calmly. Turning to his staff, he said, "Gather up what information you already have on this theory and process the raw files into readable information. The authorities will be here soon, I need to prepare procedural and conduct reports. What are you waiting for?" he asked. "GO!"

They scurried away clutching their files, exchanging worried glances. Who could have predicted that the comet would explode the moment they received the information? It was far too coincidental.

Mr Chang's heart hammered furiously as he walked the corridors leading to the main entrance. On the outside he looked calm and steady which is exactly what he needed to portray if he was to make it past the security guards.

He flashed his ID and tried to walk through the turnstile.

"We are in lock down, sir. No one goes in, no one goes out. Orders from General Bek," said the guard looking uncomfortable.

Mr Chang had been expecting this to happen at some stage and had devised a cunning contingency plan.

With perfect timing a siren began to peal at a deafening pitch.

"Fire detected in warehouse number two. Commence emergency evacuation procedures," announced an automated voice.

The people standing close by looked panic stricken. Everyone who worked in the building knew that warehouse number two was where all the hydrazine rocket propellant was stored. A fire in there was very bad news.

No one knew what to do or whether standard safety procedures should be adhered to as normal. Everyone including the security guards manning the doors had no other choice than to look to Mr Chang for direction.

"I need access to your console," he told the guard.

He moved aside at once to make room for the director. From his inner pocket Chang found his ear piece and put it back into position. Almost immediately it beeped, flashing a brilliant blue. A stream of steady chatter flowed the moment he answered.

"Take Pei, Shao, Qian and Ngo and see if the fire is small enough to be contained. I will alert provincial fire services and take steps to evacuate the rest of the complex," Chang ordered.

"You!" he said sharply to the guard. "Yes, you! Message General Bek and ask him for permission to evacuate."

The guard attempted to take control of the security console by sliding his big bulk alongside Chang's. But the director was having none of it.

"What do you think you're doing?" he said looking down his nose imperiously.

Although he was half his size, he didn't budge an inch.

"I was going to contact General Bek, just as you asked sir," he said, looking decidedly cowed. The tag on his lapel said his name was Meng.

"Well then use your ear piece you muscle bound halfwit! Can't you see I'm using the console?"

"Of course. My apologies," muttered the guard whose name was Meng.

Hastily he pulled out his ear piece and tried to put a call through to the General.

Chang supressed a smile of satisfaction as he blocked the call with a quick swipe of his finger across the touchscreen.

"The General is not answering," Meng said with a frown. "Should I try again?"

"Proceed," Chang replied glibly.

Once again the guard's message was thwarted.

"What should we do?" he asked in a pleading voice.

Chang threw an arm around his shoulder in what he hoped was a reassuring gesture.

"We shall obey the only orders we have been given regarding such an event and if anyone asks you why you acted in such a way, tell them that director Chang told you to follow CNSA orders to the letter. That is all we can do – follow standard protocol and evacuate."

"But what if the traitor escapes? What then?" argued the guard. Chang could see he was quaking in his size fourteen boots.

"Between you, I and the other guards, that's not going to happen. Our lives depend on it."

This seemed to mollify him. He even managed a little smile and a nod. A sure sign that he felt as though they were on the same team.

Good! thought Chang. That was just what he wanted. Things were going as planned even though it had been a little sticky for a while.

Behind him a door opened with a bang as hundreds of staff members filed out and headed straight for the exit.

"Halt!" the director shouted.

Everyone froze.

"Assembled on the tennis courts and hidden in various

locations along the way are a team of veteran snipers. I do not doubt that somewhere amongst you there exists a traitor to the noble ideal that is China. But fear not! That ingrate will be caught if not shot before our very eyes. One false move, my friends, and you will be a meal for the wolverines and vultures. Mark my words. Now MOVE!" he bellowed.

As though powered by a jolt of electric everyone surged forward and made their way to the tennis courts.

The area between it and the building was extensively landscaped in a bid to appease investors about the environmental impact. That meant that there was indeed ample cover for snipers or any insurgents that made it their aim to pick off the stragglers.
No one wanted to fall behind or get stranded from the rest. Moving as one they rushed towards the recreational facilities as though it was some mysterious Mecca.

"Meng," shouted Chang suddenly. "Pursue that suspect."

He was gesticulating wildly towards some bushes. Meng looked confused. He'd seen no suspect. But not wanting to appear any more incompetent than he already did, he went off to investigate.

"I'll see if I can head him off from the opposite side," said Chang snatching up a rifle. Meng nodded and melted into the dense shrubbery.

Fifteen long minutes later a motorcade of government vehicles pulled up and out stepped General Bek and his men.

They found the entire staff of CNSA still standing on the tennis courts knee deep in snow, shivering violently from the cold.

The breath of three hundred and twenty frightened scientists, office workers, janitors and guards billowed above the huge enclosure like little puffy clouds.

"Where is Mr Chang?" the General called out so that all could hear.

There were a few moments of uncomfortable silence then a petite female guard stepped forward.

"He and the chief of security, Mr Meng went after a suspect. They went that way," she said pointing.

"Really?" said the general looking tense. "How long ago?"

"Fifteen minutes, maybe a little longer."

"Fan out," he told his men. "And if you see Meng and Chang shoot them on sight. They must be stopped before they reach the port. That will be their goal. Set up road blocks on every major outlying road. They must not get away."

Suddenly his radio crackled with static.

"We've found Meng already, sir. He's been shot. Self-inflicted by the look of it," said one of the soldiers who had been searching the area.

"Good! That will make things much simpler then," said the general with a smile. "Now we just have one man to catch."

No sooner had the words left his mouth than the building behind him exploded outwards in an enormous fireball that stretched hundreds and hundreds of feet into the sky.

Ten miles away Mr Chang looked up at the towering inferno as he boarded the boat that would take him to New York. Never again would he be able to set foot in his own country. It was time to embrace the winds of change.

Chapter Twenty One

Reflections

GOD STARED AT the screen in shock and felt very much alone. Here was something that had the potential to hurt him, something that threatened the very nature of who he was. If only he could share the burden with someone, explain to them the gravity of what had just occurred. But he couldn't.

They would know then of his deception and that would alter the balance of everything. All that he had created would fall apart one atom at a time like a house of cards.

He smiled wistfully at the thought of cards. The games he and Nick played with Gabriel had become one of the few pleasures he still enjoyed. Times had indeed changed.

Ah, those were the day, he thought nostalgically. The Romans had originally been the ones to stir up their interest in games of chance. They were as obsessed with gambolling as they were with war fare.

Not only that they were incredible dutiful people, obsessed with honouring the deities. Contrary to popular belief it didn't matter to him that they had many, they were all one and the same – just different incarnations of himself.

He had rewarded their devotion with even more wealth and success. Theirs was the first world power that he'd fallen in love with and in his opinion none had matched it since for grandeur and magnificence.

Things were so much simpler then. They knew their place and were content with staying in the vicinity of the earth. But right at this particular moment in time he had trouble even identifying which world power even had supremacy, because things were changing so rapidly. Man seemed determined to oust him from his position and reach for the stars.

No, he mused, shaking his head. There were some things he just couldn't allow. It was time to contain the situation.

Turning away from the view screen he did something that he rarely ever did. He stretched out his mind and left the spiritual plain of existence.

With no discernible presence he had returned to his most basic form – an invisible field of energy that contained all that he was. In the cold vacuum of space he appeared alongside the comet to inspect what damage those troublesome humans had done.

He was in for quite a shock.

The explosion had caused the comet to split in three directions and all that was holding it together was a thin film of ice and a piece of fused Titanium. The titanium had come from the probe that the Chinese had sent, which was what had caused the explosion in the first place. Titanium and Trivarium were a deadly combination.

From what he could see there was still enough of it there to cause further trouble if it came into contact with another seam of Trivarium or one of the other rare earth elements that the comet was made up of.

That threat of another explosion gave him an idea that might just stave off disaster. But before he could begin he had to retrace the journey of the comet all the way back its birth place – deep in the heart of the Oort cloud.

Chapter Twenty Two

More Reflections

"SO YOU'RE AN angel then," said Carlos flatly. It was more a statement than a question.

"Do you doubt me?" Sarah asked watching him carefully. All these years she had wondered what he looked like. Now she knew.

He was tall from what she could tell, as he was still lying on the ground. His hair was thick and soft looking, like black lamb's wool. Instantly, she wondered why her mind had made that analogy. Father Ramirez was no black sheep. Maybe a little lost, perhaps.

His hands were, strong looking. Tanned like the rest of him and partially covered in dark hair. She had known that even when she was blind as she'd touched them by accident one day when he'd helped her carry some food baskets into the kitchen. The memory of that day made her heart skip a beat.

She looked away, glad that he could not read her thoughts.

"Of course I believe you," Carlos told her. As he watched

the breeze ruffle her dark shoulder length hair a disquieting thought suddenly occurred to him.

"Can you read people's thoughts?" he asked casually.

"No. Else I would not have needed to ask if you believed me just now," she said, reminding him of his previous question.

"Oh yes," he nodded, feeling a little silly for having asked. How strange that they would be wondering the same thing about each other, Sarah thought. Was there some sort of connection between them?

Over by the pile of boulders Casey was turning the chicken on an improvised spit fashioned from the spoke of a discarded bicycle. It smelt delicious and periodically he was tearing bits off and stuffing them in his mouth when he thought they weren't looking.

Just as Carlos got to wondering who he was and why Sarah was with him, they heard the sound of a speeding car heading in their direction.

The last thing he expected Sarah to do was pull out a glock from the back of her trousers and position herself so that she would have a clear shot should they pull up round the back of the gas station. But that was exactly what she did.

Heaven had changed her in unexpected ways, he thought to himself.

But there was no need for them to have been concerned. The car never even slowed. It just simply carried on its way throwing up dust to the throbbing beat of Saturday Night Fever which was blaring loudly from its speakers.

All three looked relieved. Casey returned to his al fresco cooking and Sarah tried once more to renew the rapport she'd once had with Carlos back when they'd both been human.

"You have changed," he commented, his eyes searching her face.

"So have you. It's the nature of life. Here let me see that leg," she said crouching at his feet. He had hurt his leg whilst struggling with Fernando.

"Can you heal me?" he asked with childlike eagerness. A miracle would be very faith affirming he decided. He sincerely hoped she would oblige. Little did he know it was not that simple.

"I was never sanctioned to use my powers that way. And I'm in human form now, so I'm not sure it could even work."

"Surely, Sarah you have not forgotten the teachings of the Lord Jesus? Although it seems most convenient for me to say so at this moment in time I must draw your attention to the occasion when he asked his opposers, 'which one of you has a son or an ox that falls into a well and will not draw it out on the Sabbath day?' As the proverb says, if it is in the power of your hand to do good then you should do it," Carlos said.

The moment he finished saying it he was struck by feelings of hypocrisy. Who did he think he was a man of his current disposition preaching to an angel? She sighed and looked away. To Carlos she appeared sad. He wondered why.

"It wasn't meant as a reproof, Sarah, just a reminder. That's all," he said affectionately. He winced as pain shot through his leg.

"I will try," she promised looking up at him earnestly. He nodded in agreement and tried to stay still as she stretched out her hand above the contusion.

She closed her eyes and muttered a silent appeal to God.

"Lord, God and Almighty Father, you have already seen fit to answer one prayer with regard to this good man, but if it pleases you, I beg that you will grant us yet another and that he may be healed by the power that you have granted me. Amen."

She tried for several minutes but frustratingly nothing happened.

"Hey," he said gently. "Don't let this get to you. You tried and for that I am grateful."

She flashed him a self-depreciating smile and contented herself instead with finding something she could use as a splint. While he waited for her to return he amused himself with watching the bats fluttering above their heads.

"You know Sarah from before I'm guessing?" Casey commented, handing him a chicken leg. The skin was crisped nicely and the meat juicy and tender. He took a bite, finding it still scalding hot, so he huffed and puffed with his mouth partway open until it had cooled enough to eat.

"Yes," he said in between chewing and blowing. "We served at the same convent – at least until she died."

"She's pretty hot eh?" said Casey with a licentious grin. Carlos glanced at his chicken as though unsure of if he was referring to that or Sarah.

"Don't give me that!" laughed Casey. "I've seen the way you look at her!"

Carlos blinked in confusion.

"It would appear you are quite misguided," he said with exaggerated calm. "Sarah and I have both taken a vow of celibacy therefore any such feelings must stay strictly that – just feelings."

"So you do have feelings for her!" crowed Casey.

"I did not say that!" protested Father Ramirez, doing his best to wipe the chicken grease off his hands. One sticky situation was bad enough!

"When you two have finished arguing, someone needs to turn that chicken. It's going black on one side," said Sarah stepping out from behind the pile of boulders. Her face was uncharacteristically flushed and it was not from the heat of the fire.

How much of the conversation had she overheard? And was the redness of her face due to anger, embarrassment or exertion?

Father Ramirez hoped it was the latter. He would have to take care in future when talking with that companion of hers. He was a tricky one. It didn't take a psychoanalyst to see that he'd got a kick out of making them both uncomfortable. What manner of acquaintance was he? And was he too an angel?

"I'm going to need some help putting his leg in a splint," she said.

In front of her were the things she'd gathered to make the crude immobiliser. Most of it was from the cork tree, such as the sheets of bark and the long fibrous roots.

Casey supported his leg whilst Sarah did her best to make the leg immobile. Throughout the procedure Carlos silently thanked the Lord that he was one of the more traditional priests who favoured long flowing robes as opposed to dog collar and slacks. The thought of having to take off his trousers in front of Sarah made his toes curl.

By the time they were done it was nearly dusk and the temperature was beginning to fall away sharply.

The dull ache of pain and the heat of the camp fire was

enough to make Carlos dose. Whilst he slept Sarah and Casey fell into an easy going conversation about this and that, intentionally avoiding anything too taxing.

They both agreed that being able to experiencing the ordinary things that they'd taken for granted just a few years ago felt good. They had thought these things would never be within reach again, that simple things such as eating a meal or taking a shower were relics of the past. They were glad to find that this was not necessarily true.

For them it was an especially poignant moment indeed to watch violet hour slowly fade as the dawn gave way to the day. The light of the fire bought out the spark in their eyes and raised a healthy glow to their cheeks that had never been there before.

Two whole hours went by without either one mentioning God or their 'other' existence. Instead they talked about their former lives. The lives that they had lead before meeting each other. Sarah listened carefully and without judgement as he related his descent into drug addiction.

He explained as best he could the moment of freedom that came with a drug induced high. Whilst under the influence he no longer felt crushed and shackled by the manacles of anger and hate instead he felt as free as a bird soaring on outstretched wings, with nothing to hold him back from doing what he wanted.

There were other things that he loved too, things that she would never have even suspected. Such as his childhood preoccupation with boats.

He told her that he thought it stemmed from a lullaby his mother had always sung to them when they were small. He couldn't remember much of it now but he knew it was about a little boy who wanted to find the island of eternal youth so that he would never have to grow up. But in order to get there he had to conquer his fear of water and climb into a little red row boat then sail across the ocean blue.

"I used to spend hours making model boats at the children's home – trying out different materials and testing their seaworthiness in the big tin bath. Back then government funding was tight, so everyone at the home shared the same bathroom. As you can imagine this didn't make me too popular wither the staff or the kids," he told her. As they talked two moths flew down low over the fire – drawn by its beacon of light.

"I suppose my childhood was quite an unconventional one when you think about it," Sarah said stretching out lazily.

"Funny you should say that," commented Casey. "The word unconventional has the word convent in it. Bit of a giveaway."

"Well, we're not all as smart as you," she said playfully.

He looked at her in mock surprise.

"Was that a compliment or did my ears deceive me?"

Chapter Twenty Three

Conversations with a Tumbleweed

"STOP WHAT YOU'RE doing and come with me," Martin said with a strange intensity. The director of NASA led Austin hurriedly down the corridor, talking animatedly on the way.

"You'll never believe who immigration officials just tagged disembarking a cargo ship from China," he said holding open a door.

"Who?" Austin asked. His mind had automatically come up with a very obvious answer but it seemed too ridiculous to say.

"Our very own Mr Chang, that's who," replied Martin. He opened a side door and grinned at the man seated in the centre of the room.

Mr Chang looked a lot older than Austin had imagined. If he had been asked to describe his general appearance he would have said he looked a bit battle worn and forlorn around the eyes. What had he been through to get here? Austin could only guess.

"I'm assuming he speaks English?" he asked Martin setting his coffee cup on the desk.

The director looked at him blankly.

"I don't know. I haven't spoken to him yet. I was waiting till you got here."

The air conditioning kicked in with a dull thump, circulating the cloying, stale air through its innards in an effort to purify and cool it. It was always unbearably hot out here on Merrit Island at the height of the summer months. Austin cleared his throat and pulled up a chair. He straddled it back to front and thrust out a hand.

"Hi! I'm Austin Harris. Chief of operations here at NASA," he said brightly.

At first he got no response. Mr Chang, if that's who he really was just stared dumbly at his proffered palm.

Perhaps there had been some sort of mix up and this is the wrong guy, thought Austin. Sure there were bound to be thousands of Mr Chang's in China, but something about the timing of all this just seemed far too coincidental. He tried again. Persistence had always been one of his defining characteristics.

"Look I'm sorry no one has spoken to you up until now. We've just been really busy with this cometary situation," he said shaking his hand as though he were an old friend. "We're not really sure what to make of it but that's no excuse for bad manners."

Chang's eyes lit up as though someone had flicked a switch.

"Ah! Yes! Ison. That's why I'm here," he said with a slow enigmatic smile. "Ison is my lucky star – my ticket to America."

Martin looked sceptical.

"Does he know anything about the comet or not?" he

whispered in Austin's ear. "I'd have thought he'd be busting his guts to tell us what he knows."

"I think he does," said Austin loudly enough for everyone in the room to hear. "He's just making sure he's talking to the right people, aren't you Mr Chang?"

"Please! Call me Xi," he said politely.

"I'm assuming you've eaten and slept since your journey?" Martin asked.

"No. I asked to be brought straight here. What I have to tell you is a matter of great urgency," Chang replied.

That made both men sit up and listen closely. Martin's fingers were suddenly a blur as he made an internal call.

"Veronica, bring something up for Mr Chang to eat please," he said.

"Right away, sir. Anything in particular?"

"Noodles?" he asked William. William nodded.

"A bowl of noodles and some chicken," he told her. "Oh, and a couple of bottles of water."

"Ok. On my way," she replied.

"So what is this matter of great urgency that you mentioned earlier?" he said turning his attention to Xi.

He tried to appear relaxed in order to put him at ease. They needed to know what the Chinese had discovered and he was their only lead.

"First I need to know that you're not going to send me back. My people do not take traitors kindly," he said.

"As you know, we've already negotiated a deal with the President. If you tell us everything you know about that comet, American citizenship is as good as yours," Martin said pulling a sheaf of papers from his brief case. He handed them to Mr Chang as proof and indicated the relevant passages.

From beneath his jagged black fringe his dark eyes scanned the page. It didn't take Mr Chang long to see that the wording was in order. Deciding whether or not it was all above board was a bit more difficult. He had no way of knowing if they would indeed follow through with their promises. All he could do was keep his end of the bargain and hope they would uphold theirs.

"Ison has split into three pieces," he told them, sitting back in his chair. He said it with an odd finality as though it was the end of the world or something.

"What? How?" Austin demanded, his brow furrowed in consternation. "What did they do?"

"They didn't do anything. Not intentionally."

"Bullshit," muttered Martin.

"So how did this happen then? Do you even know?" Austin asked.

He was doing his best to sound calm but even he felt indignant that the Chinese had taken it upon themselves to blow up the comet. How dare they destroy something that they never even had any claim on? It belonged to everyone.

"I know what you must be thinking," said Xi. "You think we did this – that we sent a probe packed with explosives and blew it up. But we didn't. It was designed just to take samples, analyse their content and send the reports back to earth. We were just as surprised as you when it exploded. In fact our government believed it was sabotage at first – committed by the West, most likely the US."

"Well as you can see it's not. Else why would we be sitting

here questioning you about it at the behest of the President?" Martin replied.

"Very true" Xi admitted with an emphatic nod.

"So are you going to tell us who did it then?" Martin said growing a little impatient.

"No one did it. It was merely the result of a chemical reaction. What you have to understand here is that when you're sending a probe hundreds of thousands of miles into space you have no way of knowing what it may encounter. Not with any great certainty anyway. Up until now, any comet that we have been able to explore has been made up of carbon, ice and gas in the main. Nothing, remotely volatile. But this comet is not like all the other ones. They came from the spherical outer part of the Oort Cloud at the edge of the solar system, whereas Ison is from the central disc shaped part of the Oort Cloud. A completely unknown region. This is the first time we've been able to get out hands on anything from that region. We should have realised that the composition would be probably different. After all the central part of the Oort cloud is a by-product of the sun exchanging materials with other nearby stars at the early stages of their formation. It has the potential to contain some very interesting elements."

Austin looked thoughtful. He was beginning to see where Xi was going with this.

"That's where the problem arose. Because we did not foresee that there may be unusual elements on Ison we could not have known that they had the potential to interact with the materials we used to construct the probe," Xi explained.

"Either that or someone sneaked a shit load of semtex on board," said Martin folding his arms sceptically. "From where I'm sitting this is beginning to sound suspiciously like a case of Ockham's razor."

"I'm not familiar with Ockham's razor," replied Xi.

"A very old principle of logic devised by a man called William Ockham. It basically means that when faced with challenging mystery often the simplest explanation is the correct one," explained Martin. "I say someone blew her up."

"Yes, but we all know of instances when that doesn't necessarily apply," Austin interjected. "And I'm hazarding a guess that this is one of those occasions. Am I right, Mr Chang?"

"Right," he said, looking a little weary. "The explosion was triggered by the combined presence of Trivarium and titanium. If you examine the explosion frame by frame you will see the infrared colour spectrum follows the exact pattern for such an event – namely a vivid purple nucleus with an orange blast margin."

"Something's not right here," said Austin shaking his head. "You sent me the results of the rock sample analysis. There was no trace of Trivarium or any other rare earth element – although I appreciate that there must have been titanium, as that was what's used to construct all interplanetary space probes."

"That is what I'm saying to you! The results were incorrect, they were flawed. Nothing else known to man could have caused that blast. Only Trivarium."

"Unless it was something else, something completely unknown to man..." Austin said with a far off look in his eye.

"This is all just useless conjecture," interrupted Martin abruptly. "What we really need to do is send a manned space craft up to that comet. Find out what's really up there. Is that doable?"

The other two men looked nonplussed, but eventually

Austin spoke.

"Martin," he said cautiously. "I know that you're an eminently qualified man when it comes to science and the field of astrophysics. But I have to wonder if you realise what you're asking. Firstly there are the time constraints. Such a mission would take months, if not years to prepare for. Secondly, there is the issue of matching its velocity. That would take unbelievable amounts of fuel too achieve and even if we did manage to achieve it, that kind of environment would pose extreme hazards to anyone dumb enough to volunteer. I'm not sure there are any space suits durable enough to withstand the kind of extremes we're talking about. But you already know all this, don't you Martin?"

"Yes I do. And so do the Chinese. Yet somehow I suspect that's not going to stop them from trying to hitch a ride on that miserable hunk of rock. Am I right Xi?"

Mr Chang nodded.

"Plans were already in motion before I even left," he said. "But why?" protested Austin. "What can they possibly hope to achieve? It's a goddamn suicide mission."

"Because this could signal the start of a space age gold rush, that's why. Where there's Trivarium there's always massive deposits of Xanobium – and you know the situation at present with that old chestnut," Martin answered.

"Are you telling me this is all about armaments?" groaned Austin. The idea repulsed him. He was a man of science not warfare.

"Think about it," said Martin. "Right now, every drone, fighter jet, laser and heat seeking missile and almost any other technologically advanced weapon you care to mention finds it target using a Xanobium powered Dante's Matrix guidance system. That means whoever controls the Xanobium deposits has a serious amount of clout on the world scene."

"So we're talking about a whole new arms race," breathed Austin, looking sickly and pale.

"China will win," Xi said matter of fact.

"So what, you've decided to join the losing side?" growled Martin. "How very noble of you!"

"This is crazy Martin!" exclaimed Austin. "This is supposed to be about science – the purity of Mother Nature's cosmos. I don't want any part of this!"

He sounded panicky. The thought of being responsible for countless deaths terrified him. It was not a destiny he wanted to pursue. Even if it meant losing his job and the bank foreclosing on the expensive house he'd just bought because he couldn't keep up with the mortgage repayments, then so be it. He would not allow himself to be a cog in the mechanics of some great global killing machine powered by the raw energies that mankind hoped to rape and pillage from the solar system's only come bearing cloud!

It was disgraceful! And to think he'd got his hopes set on Mr Chang being some kind of Eastern Messiah as far as the scientific community was concerned! All he had done was stir things up. NASA had become a veritable hornet's nest since his arrival – and that was only a relatively short time ago.

"Just stop and think for a second. Can the US really allow China to hold a bigger monopoly than it already has on Xanobium? They already control the majority of the rare earth elements deposits here on earth. What do you think will happen if they gain access to even more? It will swing the entire balance of power in their favour. And if you think that's a good thing, wake up and ask yourself why tens of thousands of people like Mr Chang are leaving their country in droves every year and coming here," said Martin, trying to appeal to his sense of reason.

This seemed to have the desired effect. Austin was obviously considering what he had said and making the right connections.

"He's right you know. That's the reason why I came to you with this. A world in which one country exercises dominion over the rest would be a dangerous place to live. There has to be a balance of power and a sharing of humanity's resources, else all you've got is a global dictatorship," said Xi.

"Listen to him," Martin said. "He knows what he's talking about."

Just then Veronica entered the room carrying a tray. The chicken and noodles smelt divine making Austin wish that he'd ordered some himself.

"Just set that down on the table please," said Martin curtly, hoping to expedite her exit.

She looked a bit affronted by his manner so he softened the blow by calling out his thanks as she left.

"If we do this, it's going to make a lot of people very unhappy," said Austin. "They're not just going to let us fly up to the Ison and take everything."

"Let's get one thing straight here," Martin said. "Firstly it's not if we do this, it's when we do this and mark my words it will be sooner rather than later. I haven't spoken to the Presidential advisors yet, but I'm one hundred per cent certain what they will say. Secondly, this is not just about Ison. It's about where it

214

originated from – this Oort cloud. Ison is just a rather large nugget from what I can see. What we really need to do is get our hands on the gold mine itself – the Oort Cloud, before anyone else gets their hands on it. Stake our claim as it were."

Austin looked as though he was beginning to come round to the idea. But he appeared to have further questions.

"One thing I'm just wondering here," he said. "And maybe you could help me with this Xi. How come the probe sent back dodgy data? Were the results falsified to throw us of the scent?"

"Well if they were, it wasn't by us. It threw us off the scent too."

"I'm not sure I believe that. Somebody knew. Maybe they intercepted the signal somehow," Martin postulated.

He paused for a moment to let the implications of that statement sink in.

"So someone knows what's up there and doesn't want us to get our hands on it," he continued.

"But who?" asked Austin.

"Well, that's the trillion dollar question isn't it?" said Martin. "I can see a war brewing here fellas if we're not too careful."

Chapter Twenty Four

Stirring

FROM ISAKAR'S POSITION he could see nothing out the ordinary going on. He was flying in mid-heaven looking for signs of what could be troubling God. He was the Devil's chief agent – his right hand man so to speak. It was his job to work behind the scenes and find out everyone's dirty little secrets. To discover what lay hidden. To watch and observe, then report back to his master.

Discovering God's secrets was never an easy task. So far he'd had little success in finding anything out but he hoped that this would soon change. He had a feeling that a breakthrough was imminent. All he had to do was keep his eyes and ears open.

For a while he had wondered whether the issue was anything to do with the massive cyclone that was about to make landfall on the southern coast of Australia or the small pox outbreak in India. After a day or too he was able to rule them both out. And it was definitely nothing to do with Sarah and Casey bumping into Carlos Ramirez. He knew that He'vernon had visited God to warn him about that very issue and that he had been far too busy to care.

That had all the hallmarks of the Devil's intervention actually. Isakar snickered, amused in the knowledge that he had engineered the meeting between Sarah and Carlos without God so much as blinking an eyelid. It was obvious what he hoped to achieve through his actions. The chemistry between Carlos and Sarah had always been palpable, even back when she'd been blind. Whether or not they'd fall into the trap he'd set for them remained to be seen.

Perhaps they needed a little encouragement, thought Isakar. So just to be helpful he focused his powers on the little tin can of a car that they were travelling in as it sped along the dusty roads. With a little tweak here and there he greatly increased the speed of the combustion process so that it used up all its fuel before they reached the next gas station.

"Oh fuck!" growled Casey as the car began to cough and slowly grind to a halt. "We've run out of fuel."

"Give it a minute then try starting it again," suggested Carlos.

Sarah was too distracted by Father Ramirez's condition to complain over his use of foul language. His leg was not as bad as she had first thought but she could not shake off the memory of how they had found him. It was his emotional wellbeing that now concerned her.

There was an air of anxiety about him - a dissatisfaction with all that he encountered. Life did not sit well with him anymore. There was something was very wrong. She shuddered at the thought of finding him with the gun lodged in his mouth – milliseconds from taking his life. He was in a bad place – that much she knew. Her being there was making it worse. In order to avoid encroaching on his personal space she'd huddled up in the corner over by the window. If only she knew what was wrong. If only she knew what he needed. Secretly she wanted to be his everything but she felt as though she shouldn't be there.

Casey followed his suggestion and the car purred into life. They travelled a few hundred yards before it kangarooed violently and stalled catapulting both Sarah and Carlos forward. The next thing Sarah knew she was lying on her back looking into the concerned face of Father Ramirez.

"Are you all right?" he said.

She tried to sit up, but her head was too painful. She must have hit it when the car lurched forward. That must have been some bump she thought, touching the lump on her forehead gingerly.

"So much for having human bodies..." she said wincing.

Casey turned the engine over once more. But it was a pointless exercise. The tank was empty.

"How can we have run out of fuel?" she asked. "We had three quarters of a tank when we started off. We haven't driven that far."

"How should I know? It's just a thirsty car for its age I guess," he said.

He got out of the car and popped open the trunk. Curious as to where he was going she sat up with Carlos's help.

"Are you ok?" he asked once more. Sarah suppressed a smile. He really did seem concerned about her.

Although she was now in sitting up he seemed reluctant to let her go. His hands must have healing powers, she thought. Her pain was magically melting away – either that or his touch was a distraction from it. Little did she know that she was having the same effect on him. His proximity to her was like a balm to his troubled soul.

"I'm just a little dizzy," she told him.

"Here, put your head on my shoulder if that helps."

Hesitantly she followed his suggestion. Closing her eyes, she wondered at the unusual pace of her heart. It seemed to be trying it's best to leap out of her chest. She gave a deep sigh in order to calm herself unaware that the quaking pulse in his neck quickened at the feel of her warm breath caressing his bare throat.

"Found a fuel can," Casey called. In the rear view mirror she could see him holding up a lime green can.

"I wonder which of us is going to draw the short straw and make the walk to the next gas station," Sarah murmured to Carlos. Her head hung low and her lips almost touched his ear when she spoke. It sent a heady thrill through Carlos's veins that was impossible to deny.

"I'm not leaving you," he said firmly.

The way he said it made Sarah's chest ache. She didn't want him to leave either. Not now. Not ever. She knew that she was being irrational but she wanted him to hold her this way forever. Heaven could wait. Perhaps Casey would step up and make the journey for fuel. Surely he would see that that was best.
He walked around the side of the car and rapped on the window. Sarah wound it down and gazed up at him – her eyes pleading for him to go in her stead. He gave her a strange look. The way she was looking at him gave him the shivers.

The last time anyone had looked at him like that he'd done terrible things and looking back on it all now he wasn't even sure why. It was just there – an inexplicable need to subjugate and hurt, a ravenous anger that required blood to sate it. Even now it was still there, smouldering away in some forgotten corner of his mind. Only now its nature had changed.

"Well you two look pretty cosy in there," he said peering through the window.

Carlos looked a bit uncomfortable.

"She's feeling dizzy," he said by way of explanation.

"I bet she is," Casey said with a knowing wink. Sarah scowled, then winced in pain. Carlos felt her flinch and searched her face with a worried expression.

"I'm ok, really," she said trying to reassure him.

"Well, I'm going to leave you two love birds to it and go get some fuel," said Casey straightening up.

"But we don't have any money," she said.

"You let me worry about that," he replied looking off into the distance.

"Here. I've got money," said Carlos, passing him a bunch of crumpled pesos. "Don't want you robbing anyone just to get us some fuel."

Casey grinned. "Whatever gave you that idea?"

"Nothing. Just call it intuition," nodded Carlos.

"Whatever," laughed Casey slapping the roof of the car with his palm. "See you shortly."

He walked away with a smile pasted across his face. But as is often the case when a person sets off on a solitary walk he soon fell into a reflective mood. He found himself feeling envious that Sarah had someone who obviously missed her. In the past relationships were not something he'd bothered with and for good reason. They seemed too much like hard work with not enough rewards. He preferred to just take what he wanted - to hell with the rest. He would be the first to admit he had lived an utterly selfish life fuelled by bitterness and hatred. It had been quite a ride. But where had it got him? And had it really taken strength to act that way? He was beginning to see that holding on to his anger all these years had been a poison chalice. He had thought that he was truly happy, just pleasing himself and doing whatever he wished. But was he really?

There were so many things that he'd never experienced, although he'd taken plenty through rape, robbery and murder. The thought of having earned the privilege of being physically and emotionally close to someone now looked like the more desirable option rather than the booby prize.

All he'd ever done was hurt and kill and the result was a gaping hole where an ordinary life should be. How ironic that he Casey Davenport, career criminal extraordinaire, felt robbed. The question was who was to blame? He'd always thought he was in control of his own life and to a large extent he was – but there were events in his life that had had a definite impact on him, for the worse, like ripples spreading outwards on a pond. Those he had no control over.

As he thought about this his anger built – he had to know where ultimate culpability lay and not just for his train wreck of a life. There were many others like him. The world was full of them. He thought again about the analogy of the pond with the ripples spreading outwards from where a stone had been thrown in. His mind was searching, searching for the stone that had caused the ripples in the first place, the hand that had thrown it or the mind that had searched out the pebble that had been hurled in the first place.

A flash of light suddenly sparked within his brain; an epiphany as it were. He was the stone, Cal, his father had thrown him and the pond was maelstrom that had been his life so far. The ripples were all the people he'd ever connected with – rushing to flee from chaos he created.

He trudged along purposefully hoping that out there, not too far away was another gas station – one that was operational. He had a dead nun and a half dead priest to rescue. No doubt they were sitting back there wondering if they could really trust him to return as most people would in their situation. They had after all given him money, a gun and he even had a brand new body. It was like a cross road lay before him.

On the one hand here was his chance to do something good of his own volition or he could continue being selfish just as he'd always been and the loose the only human connection he'd had in decades. That choice would not have been difficult for the old Casey. He would have been over the green woods and far away before you could say cocaine. He was a different person now though. It had taken three years to get to where he was and the change had been painful. He knew he didn't have to do this. But he wanted to. He wanted to help Sarah in whatever way he could because he felt grateful for her perseverance. He'd already bought her down to earth with him so that she could help Carlos against God's express command. That was quite a risk and there was no saying how that was going to turn out.

Now he was giving up potential freedom for her, the chance to start afresh. It could work out very badly. But he had faith that no matter what the repercussions were for him the good that would come from his selfless deed would spread outwards like the ripples on a pond. It would be like a negative image of everything he'd ever done before. He pressed on, determined to ring in the changes.

Back at the car Sarah was beginning to shiver. She struggled to prevent her teeth from chattering.

"Are you cold or is it the pain?" asked Carlos.

"Both," she said untruthfully.

Her head wasn't very sore at all now. The elation she felt at being so close to him had diminished it to just a dull ache. It was that same elation that was making her tremble. Perhaps talking would take her mind of it.

"Carlos," she said. "I was wondering. How did it come about that you ended up here in Mexico City?"

He smiled awkwardly.

"I became dissatisfied with life at the convent. I decided it was time to move on. Start somewhere new," he told her.

He sounded sad. The memory of how he felt when Sarah died still haunted him. She had slipped through his fingers before he had even had a chance to tell her how he felt. The problem was he'd taken too long to admit that he loved her. Yet here she was. Before him was a second chance, if only he was brave enough to take it. Acknowledging this was one thing; doing something about it was another.

As though sensing his inner turmoil Sarah reached out and gently took his hand as though to calm him. She held it between her own small palms and looked up at him intently, her eyes shining with an inner brightness that had not been there before.

"I wish I had been there for you Carlos," she said. "I am sorry."

Her apology took him aback.

"No one can apologise for dying Sarah," he told her. "It's a part of our life. We're born. We live. We die. We have no control over it."

"No we don't," agreed Sarah.

The warmth of her hands was spreading to his through their skin to skin contact. The thought of it made him feel flushed. He looked away to hide his embarrassment.

"Did he ever tell you why he took you?" he said suddenly. Straight away she knew he meant God. The source of his discontentment now became clear. If only she could somehow dispel it, but she had nothing to tell him. No comfort to offer because she too was struggling with similar issues.

"This is not an easy subject Carlos," she said carefully.

"No it is not," he said with a sigh. "But if you have answers I need you to share them. My faith is no longer the fortress it used to be. It's in danger of crumbling completely if I don't find some way to restore it."

"I wish I could help you. But I'm afraid I'm no better off myself."

"I don't understand!" said Carlos looking bewildered.

"My faith is probably just as shaky as yours right now," she told him, "maybe more so. I've seen first-hand the way things are and how God runs things. And I'm not the only one struggling to make sense of it."

"What do you mean? How can you have doubts? He's real! You've seen him. You live in heaven Sarah! You get to talk to him don't you? I haven't had the luxury of any of that. None of us down here have and yet we're expected to just accept all the crap that goes on down here under the umbrella explanation of 'it's God's will'. Well I don't buy into that anymore. I just want to know why he took you from me!"

By the time he had finished he was shaking. Sarah didn't quite know what to say. She'd never ever expected to hear him say those things and there was no mistaking what he meant.

"I've upset you," he said watching her closely. She stared off into the distance trying to make sense of what he'd just told her.

"I'm sorry Sarah," he said, his voice tinged with regret. He wished he could take his words back. They were obviously too much for her – perhaps they were too much for him.

"Sarah, I…"

Suddenly she turned and clung to him tightly pressing her face into his chest. His breath hitched at this rather unexpected development.

"Have I hurt you?" she said pulling back a little. He shook his head dumbly.

"Good," she murmured, then kissed him softly on the lips. Her touch was like a feather. It was gentle and reserved at first then becoming more insistent as their passion grew. It was hard to know where love began and lust ended. The two emotions were inseparable for them. They had been denied for far too long.

"How is this even possible?" whispered Carlos, coming up for air.

"I don't know and I don't care. Just shut up and kiss me," replied Sarah, grazing his bottom lip with her teeth.

This only served to inflame his ardour even more. He clasped her waist with his trembling hands and hoisted her onto his lap determined never to let her go until she understood what she meant to him.

Life had taught him the error of missing such opportunities. For all he knew this chance may never come again. With this in mind he looked into her eyes and was overjoyed to find that she returned his gaze with equal intensity that spoke of something much deeper than a passing attraction.

All else quickly faded into insignificance until they were rudely interrupted by a loud honking noise.

"Come on you two!" Get in!" shouted Casey. He was parked alongside them in a shiny new pickup truck. Mortified that they'd been caught red handed they got in without question. Where he may have gotten the new set of wheels never entered their heads. The only thing they could think about was when they could next get time alone.

Casey took a peek at their guilty faces in the rear view mirror.

"Well, the dog collar is well and truly off I see," he smirked.

Carlos had it in his hands and was staring at it as though he was seriously considering throwing it out of the window. Sarah gently took it from him and attempted to fasten it at the back of his neck. He put up his hand to stop her.

"I am not fit to wear this anymore," he said. She looked deeply hurt. Is that how he had viewed being with her?

"Hey!" He tilted her chin up so that she had no choice but to look at him. "I meant that my personal crisis of faith makes it impossible. Not because of what happened with us."

"It will pass," she told him. "You will find your way again. Although you have not seen God himself you have seen the evidence that he exists. I am it. ME."

"I do not doubt that he exists Sarah, I doubt that he is the person mankind thinks he is. Something's not right. You alluded to this yourself."

Sarah's stomach lurched. She realised now what she had done. Before her had been a man teetering on the edge of spiritual collapse.

Instead of bolstering his faith and doing what she could to provide reassurance she had allowed her feelings for him to take over - worse still she had knocked him even further down the ladder with her own problems. He'd even begged her to perform a miracle hadn't he? He wanted to believe. Now she had given him a reason not to. If he believed in God and retained his calling what they had just done was a sin.

Priests were not able to pursue physical relationships. Twenty five minutes with her on the back seat of an old mustang had blown what little faith he'd got to smithereens.

How could she have been so selfish! This was who he was; the robes, the dog collar, the belief system. Who was she to come along and make things worse than they were already? If she loved him she would have to make it right somehow. No matter what the cost.

"Carlos," she said taking his hand in hers. "We both have to be face up to the fact that we have no future together. I must shortly go back to my realm and you will go back to being a priest. That's just the way it is whether we like it or not. I know I said some things about God but the fact is he is still the Almighty. His power is greater than we will probably ever know. And yet the connection you and I have is like nothing I've ever known but I think we both know deep down, that it can never work no matter how much we wish it."

"You want to know what I think?" said Casey surprising them both. He'd been listening to the two of them the whole time since the radio didn't work and the road ahead was straight and boring.

"What?" they both asked in unison.

"I think humans have made the mistake of thinking that power equals perfection. In fact humans have assumed far too many things about God but that's because we're so short on actual concrete facts. We have a habit of filling in the gaps. There are writings yes – but no one alive can say with absolute certainty that they came from God or that he even agrees with them."

"So like I said it's pointless believing in him," said Carlos.
"No it's not," replied Casey.

Sarah grinned. Well, well, well. This was a turn up for the books, a criminal preaching to the converted.

"None of us are perfect. I'm certainly not. But you put your trust in me when I said I was going to get fuel. My track record is not a good one, as I'm guessing Sarah has already told you. Yet you waited for me to come back…if you can call getting jiggy with it waiting. If you can trust in someone like me to make good how can you not give God the benefit of the doubt? Tell me if I'm wrong here, but isn't it quite an easy thing to put faith in something that cannot possibly let you down?"

Sarah and Carlos both nodded, intrigued by what he had to say.

"Right!" he said thumping the wheel. "It's easy for me to have faith in the sun shining above us because I'm one hundred per cent certain it will never let me down. Not in my life time. This car I'm driving, well that's a different matter. You saw what happened with the last one. They break down. Run out of fuel. All sorts of things can happen. But even so...we are still entrusting our lives to it. We climb in – aware that it may break down at any time even though its power is greater than ours. If you can entrust such flawed mechanical contraptions with your life knowing that they can and will fail, why can you not content yourself with what God has to offer humanity?"

His audience appeared to be struck dumb. So he answered the question for them.

"I'll tell you why. Because as I said at the start humanity is far too hung up on perfection, that's the truth of the matter."

"You spoke well brother," said Carlos leaning forward to grasp his shoulder. He had been unexpectedly moved by what Casey had to say.

Suddenly, the back window imploded and three .357 Magnum bullets ploughed into the back of his head. To say there was not much left of his features when they were done was an understatement. A frightful mound of scarlet mush held together by glistening fragments of bone, teeth and sinew teetered atop his trembling shoulders in a grim mimicry of life. It was a vile, vile lie, one that had Sarah screaming till she thought her lungs would burst. There was nothing either of them could do. The man she had made love to not even an hour ago was now a cold and greying corpse spilling gore upon her feet.

The car spun off the road and had now stopped at the foot of a tree. Fernando's men leapt from their cars and were hot footing it up the hill towards them.

"Sarah! Pull yourself together! They're coming. We need to go back," yelled Casey.

Sarah sank to the floor and cradled what was left of Father Ramirez, her face streaked with blood stains.

"Sarah! I cannot return without you. Please!"

She stared off into space, heedless and unknowing her eyes brimming with unshed tears.

Chapter Twenty Five

Money Versus Ethics

"WELL WE'VE GOT the go ahead to send another probe, only this time it will be carrying a payload of explosives," Martin said cautiously.

"Well that's a shitty idea if you don't mind my saying so," Austin replied looking up sharply. He'd only had two coffees that morning and he wasn't in the mood for any bullshit.

Although Martin was the director of the facility the two of them tended to have a pretty casual working relationship. They'd worked together since leaving university and most of the time they got on quite well.

Martin grinned a tad sheepishly. He could see his friend was mad. Real mad. But for him the job was king.

"Look. I get it. It just wouldn't be you if you didn't sound off about this," he said in an apologetic tone. "But you're wasting your time Austin. This decision came down from the top."

Thoroughly frustrated, Austin slammed down the lid that housed the battery unit on one of the lunar rovers. He'd been checking for signs of corrosion and had just changed the battery over to one of the newer crystalline gel versions.

"That's just typical isn't it? The bureaucrats and politicians once again get to poke their pompous fucking noses in where they're not wanted and interfere with space agency decisions. Well tell me this…do any of them have a degree in astrophysics, or quantum mechanics? I'm willing to bet my left testicle they don't. This is all about money. Cause who gives a damn about science if we can blow stuff up and make gazillions of dollars? Am I right? But that being the case I'm assuming the reverse is true. I'm sure they won't mind if I go to the Oval Office and start interfering in government legislation and protocol even though I know not one god damn thing about it! If it's lucrative why not?"

After his rant was over Austin stood in his oil stained NASA coveralls his nostrils flaring rapidly. This kind of thing really got to him. The two of them stared each other off, more like combatants in the ring than friends. It crossed his mind that he might have gone too far this time. But the way he felt about ISON and the rest of space he didn't really care if he had. To hell with it!

"Assholes!" he growled snatching up his tool box. He stormed off up the corridor and stowed it in a nearby locker. Hot on his heels, Martin followed hoping he could calm him down. He needed him on board if at all possible.

Once he caught up with him he felt unsure of how to go about defusing the situation.

"What if I told you, you will finally get your hands on a comet? Actually touch it? For real."

"Then I'd say you were nuts. Is this before or after we blow it up?"

"Neither."

"Explain," replied Austin snappily.

"Well how's about you come down off your high horse first and then we can go have a little chat in my office?"

Austin looked doubtful. He was wary of selling his soul to the Devil and that's what those pen pushers and penny counters upstairs were after.

"Come on," said Martin. "Talking doesn't cost anything."

"Ha! Tell that to Judas Iscariot. I do not intend to follow in his footsteps. The universe will not be betrayed by me. Ison is billions of years old. Who are we to come along and blow it up?"

"God damn it, Austin! How many times do I have to say this? We are not going to blow ISON up! What would be the point in that?"

"I don't know. You tell me."

"I will tell you," Martin said clamping a hand on his friend and colleagues shoulder, "over a hot cup of coffee in my office. Agreed?"

"Why not?" he replied, with a mean glint in his eye.

Chapter Twenty Six

Baby Shower

INSIDE THE OORT Cloud God sat on the humble beginnings of a brand new comet. This is where they were formed and forged from the matter that was left over from the creation of the solar system.

It would take hundreds of years for it to tear itself free from the confines of the glowing womb of the Oort Cloud before finally being able to make its way across the heavens, streaking past earth's curious inhabitants and looping its way around the sun.

Upon first discovering the Oort cloud, God had spent many years watching their progress as one would watch a piece of clay being shaped on a potter's wheel.

It was not just their formation that fascinated him. Their journey was of interest to him also. He just loved the way they blasted their way through space with their comma's or tails streaking behind them. They reminded him of the ancient phoenix legends.

He remembered the first time he'd seen a comet, back when the earth was still young – back when he himself had been young.

At that time the earth was a vastly different place, full of strange creatures and dangerous ever changing landscapes.

A good many things had evolved since then, most especially the boy who would eventually become God.

Chapter Twenty Seven

In The Beginning...

BEFORE THE ADVENT of the wheel and the appearance of religion three little boys and a young girl walked the stark middle plains of a land that would later become known as Croatia. The primitive lands around them were a dried out husk of mud, baked hard until they resembled shattered clay beneath the unrelenting heat of the sun. Sadness was etched deeply upon their hearts like a permanent scar on their otherwise youthful flesh.

Above them raptors soared on outstretched wings, their keen eyes watching for signs that they were faltering. The question was not would they survive, it was for how long.

This pitiful band of travellers had formerly belonged to a tribe known as the Hanzyek. But no more. As tradition demanded they had been ordered to leave their tribe the moment another man took their mother as his mate.

Their own father had been killed during the hunt – trampled to death beneath the hooves of a giant auroch – a breed of giant cattle that roamed the open plains

Theirs was a patriarchal society and much like the present day lion, any man of the Hanzyek tribe had license to put to death the children of another man if he became mated to their mother. If the man was of a lenient disposition he might soften the blow in order to win the woman's affections by banishing them to the hinterlands instead.

That was what had happened in this case. He've, Ab'ril, Ash'tan and Is'godt were sent off by their tearful mother with numerous packages that she had hastily put together.

She had only three days warning of the mating and so had very little time to prepare anything for her children. Casting aside her grief for the sake of the children she had worked hard to put together parcels of both fresh and cured meat in the three days freedom she still had available to her. Large prey was too much for someone of her stature so she focused instead on hunting snakes, lizards, rock badgers and rabbits. These were not difficult to take down with her well-worn sling shot and sharp eye.

Some of it she exchanged with other members of the tribe for cured meat and the skin bottles that they would need for carrying water. The others doubted that her children would survive long enough to consume any of it but they were glad of the opportunity to show their support. Their father had been a respected man and a good hunter.

It was with these meagre items that the children were to be sent out from their tribe to face the harsh reality of life out on their own. The night before they left was especially difficult. As she prepared them for their journey fear and sadness threatened to swallow her up. Before they slept in the familial bed of furs and hides for one last time their mother took Is'godt the eldest to one side –away from the others so that they could talk. She had something to say – a request to make of her first born son.

He looked up at her in the light of the flickering fire that had been set at the mouth of the cave to ward of ravenous predators. This was their home, complete with its cave paintings, glittering crystals and dusty floor. Leaving was going to be hard. His heart ached to throw his arms about her and enjoy the warmth that came with the strength of their bond. But it was not time for that. The time for that had long since passed. He was not a weanling who still snuck a feed at his mother's teat when no one was looking. He was almost nine. In three more years he would be expected to take part in his first hunt and go through the initiation ceremony that all adult males must pass before reaching manhood.

If only he was that old now. Then he could challenge the suitor by demonstrating his ability to care for the family himself. As he had not passed the initiation he was powerless to stop it. A boy of eight was not deemed old enough to provide and protect a full grown woman such as his mother.

"Is'godt, you always were an obedient boy," said his mother crouching on the dust floor of the cave.

She wanted to look him in the eye so that she could see his true feelings. From beneath his shaggy blonde hair bright blue piercing eyes peered out, both knowing and curious just as they had been at the time of his birth. Her throat tightened with unshed tears at the memory of that moment whilst behind them dancing shadows broke up the dimly lit cave with their darkness.

The rest of the tribe sat round about, deeply subdued, trying to busy themselves rather than focus on the drama playing out in the corner. They felt this was a difficult yet necessary tradition. What man would want to risk his life providing for another man's offspring? Yet whatever they felt in that regard they could not help but feel sorry for their kinswoman and her children.

Is'godt waited patiently for her to speak. It may be the last thing she ever said to him personally. He must remember it well.

"My son, there are many things you must know before you step out on to the open plains alone. If I could prevent it I would. But you know that is not possible. All I can do is forearm you with the knowledge that you will need to survive," she said in a low gravelly voice.

He nodded resolutely as she laid her hands upon his shoulders.

"Firstly, you must never, ever allow Ash'tan to take charge," she said looking him straight in the eye.

Is'godt had his suspicions why she said this but rather than question her judgement he just nodded his assent. There are some things mother's no doubt keep to themselves he thought. He respected her wisdom.

"Secondly, you must never walk out in the open after sun down. Always set up camp and if possible build a fire. Thirdly, you must always think not what's best for the minority but what is best for the majority. There's always a bigger picture and that's what counts. A true leader will know what's best for everyone, no matter what the cost."

Is'godt's heart quaked inside of him. The responsibility was too great.

"You can do this," she told him. "You were born for this. Did I ever tell you the story of your birth?" She had, many times. But he wanted to hear it again one last time so he shook his head and sat down to listen.

"For many hours you and your sister He've were stuck fast. For days in fact. The birth was the most difficult the medicine woman had ever dealt with. Neither one of you seemed ready to face the world but my body had reached the limits it could tolerate. For five days the medicine woman and I went without sleep and on the sixth day I could tell by her face that death was stalking me and my unborn twins. Just when I thought I could take no more and that my light was about to be extinguished for good you decided to make a break for it. After five big pushes you came into the world in a rush of blood and water, blinking and wide eye at the harshness of it. The strangest thing was that you still had hold of He've. You had her hand clasped in yours and you weren't about to let her go. It was the strangest thing she had ever seen the mid wife said later and she had witnessed many births. I barely had the strength to birth your sister, but that didn't matter. Because you were there. A born leader. You were the one that lead her into this world my son. I could not have done it without you. You were there to take up the short fall for my frailties and you will do the same now. It is you who will lead your sister and brothers. I have faith in you my little Godt. You will make me proud and the memory of your father will live on."

This speech seemed to drain her of all energy. She swayed with the burden of emotions that could no longer be contained no matter how hard she tried.

Is'godt got to his feet and drew himself up tall.

"I will do as you ask," he said. "You must not worry any longer."

His mother nodded.

"I know you will. We must get some rest now my son so that we can face what the morning brings with strength."

She lead him to the fur pile where his two brothers and He've were already sleeping. Taking care not to disturb them they climbed in and were immediately comforted by the warmth.

Before the sun had fully risen the next day, the children had already left the safety of the tribal cave. Unwilling to make it even harder for their mother they refrained from tears and sad faces whilst in sight of her, choosing to wait till they had travelled to the next valley.

There, He've broke down and sat crying on a rock until the other two joined in, adding their tears to her own. Is'godt felt no urge to take part. He was content to watch over them until they had finished. His feelings must remain hidden if he was to gain their respect as leader.

Their journey progressed over the coming days and their initial shock at their situation eventually subsided giving way to a dull acceptance. On the one hand this pleased him as they could make better headway but on the other he felt they were being disloyal to their mother.

At least he could be thankful that they did not question his leadership. And why would they? For it had been bestowed upon him by their mother. He decided where they should go, where they should set up camp, who should keep watch while the others slept and how often they should delve into their supplies. Even at that, these soon dwindled until their journey became punctuated by the sound of their growling stomachs.

"We must find water soon," said He've, licking her cracked lips. Twilight was approaching and the stars were starting to come out one by one. She felt glad to see them. It meant that they would stop soon and rest.

"If you had any sense you would not be wasting your energy stating the obvious," Is'godt reprimanded. He too was tired.

He've hung her head and fell silent. Although none of them spoke of it now she still felt the loss of their family and tribe keenly. Possibly more so than the others. They all recognised this apart from Is'godt.

"Here. These leaves contain a little water. Chew on these," said Ash'tan holding out a twig with three leaves attached.

"Don't give out our supplies so carelessly!" snapped Is'godt snatching away the twig from his hand.

Ashtan ground his teeth together in annoyance but said nothing. They could not afford to waste valuable energy arguing amongst themselves.

"Come! We will set up camp when we get to that second ridge," commanded Is'godt over his shoulder.

Their senses were on high alert as the land was full of shadows and strange sounds. Dead trees reached up towards the sky their leaves and fruit long since stripped away. Anything could be lurking here ready to swallow them up and tear them limb from limb at a moment's notice.

He've looked around fearfully and quickened her pace not wanting to be left behind. Suddenly she stopped and grabbed Ashtan's arm.

"Look!" she cried, pointing up towards the stars.

Ashtan followed her gaze and saw what looked like a whitish blue flame moving slowly across the heavens.

"What is it?" he breathed in an awestruck voice. He'd

never seen anything like it.

"I don't know," she said in a small voice.

The object shone as brightly as the moon ejecting a trail of incandescent vapours over forty thousand miles long. The others had noticed it now and had also stopped to marvel at its curious beauty.

"What is it?" repeated Ashtan. The others looked to Is'godt for an answer so he gave them his best guess.

"I've heard about this," he said. It is a type of giant bird that lives amongst the stars."

"It looks scary," said He've with a shudder.

Is'godt smiled at her indulgently and rested a brotherly hand on her shoulder.

"Do not worry. It will not hurt you," he told her. "Besides, legend has it that the fire bird brings good fortune for our people. It is a good sign."

"Really?" she asked. She had her head tilted up to the sky so that her eyes could drink in its glory.

"Yes. Really. Come now. We must go."

He held out his hand to her and she took it obediently. Ashtan glowered. Who did Is'godt think he was bossing them around like this? In defiance he gave one last look over his shoulder at the firebird.

"Is'godt! Look!" he cried. "Something is falling from the sky!"

"What is it?" He've whispered, in wonderment.

They stopped and watched it fall through the atmosphere, glowing ever brighter with every passing minute of its decent.

"Eggs," said Is'godt. "It must be an egg laid by the

firebird. There may be more if we keep watching."

But there wasn't. There was however a huge explosion once it hit the ground. The shock wave hit them like a slap almost bursting their ear drums. Somewhere close by a hyena howled and terrestrial birds flew off squawking in alarm. The ground rattled beneath their feet and the children fell on their faces in alarm.

He've clapped her hands over her ears and curled up in the foetal position until the mayhem had subsided.

"What in father's name was that?" breathed Ashtan.

He was the first to stand up, intrigued by the power of the event. Not wanting to be out done, Is'godt also stood up and strode forward to clip Ashtan round the ear for mentioning their father in such casual terms. But he became side tracked from his objective by the peculiarity of the air.

All around them the air fizzed like ocean surf, settling on their skin with the touch of a thousand tiny pin pricks. The four of them gazed in wonder at the glowing dust particles swirling through the air.

They sensed it was a strange event as their eyes had become unnaturally heavy, staring at the glittery fallout. The star flakes infected them with an unusual tiredness until one by one they fell where they stood, a heap of tangled limbs and scrawny bodies.

How long they slept He've could not tell but she was the first to come to. It was her unquenched thirst that roused her from her slumber. Like the ground beneath them she was parched. It was hard to swallow. They needed to find water and soon.

The sun peeped from behind the clouds, its rays already evaporating the slight dew that had fallen in the night. Seeing her chance He've drank the droplets of water that had gathered inside the huge umbrella leaves that grew here and there amongst the rocky outcrops. She became quite absorbed in her quest so that she ended up a considerable distance from the others.

Soon a call from behind told her that her disappearance had been discovered. Rather than answer she took a few steps forward upon noticing the upward curving rim of a crater about ten metres away. Something drew her towards it compelling her to ignore her brothers. Whether it was curiosity, instinct she did not know. Either way she felt compelled to follow its leadings and find out what was on the other side.

The voice behind her called again. It was Is'godt, her twin. It was not right to worry him. So she cried out loudly to let him know where she was –

"I'm here!"

"Where?" he bellowed.

"Here!" she said clawing her way up the steep edge of the crater. Once she reached the top she peered cautiously over the edge. What she saw inside took her breath away.

Chapter Twenty Eight

Discovery

A SHINING LAKE of water had collected over an unspecified period of time in the bottom of the massive crater. In the very centre was a large island shrouded in steamy vapours that seemed to be seeping from the scorched earth.

The environment there was extremely moist making it the perfect habitat for tall, lush grasses, flowers and ferns. Dense foliage covered the island as if to shield it from prying eyes whilst round about coral coloured birds similar to the modern day flamingo sifted through the shallows with their strangely fringed beaks. It certainly was an unusual place.

Suddenly, Is'godt burst through the undergrowth and bowled straight into her knocking her head over heels down the slope. Realising his error he reached out to stop her fall but in doing so he also lost his footing and rolled after her wildly flailing his arms.

The two of them came to a stop in the shallows of the water where they sat gasping, the air knocked out of them.

"What is this place?" said Is'godt, looking round.

"I don't know. But it has water," declared He've splashing her feet a little.

He held up his hands to shield himself.

"Perhaps there is food too," she said nodding towards the island.

"Yes but we don't know what's out there," Is'godt pointed out. "It may be dangerous."

"I hadn't thought of that. I wouldn't want to lead us into danger."

"Says she who wandered off on her own," he retorted.

He've bowed her head guiltily.

"It won't happen again."

"Good," he replied.

A shout from above told them that the others had found them.

"We're down here," called Is'godt. "We've found water."

The others navigated the steep incline, half climbing half tumbling and tripping. When they got to the bottom they looked around, incredulous at the oddness of it.

"What is this place?"

"I've never seen anything like it," agreed Ash'tan. He dipped his cupped hands into the water and took a few greedy gulps.

"I have not approved this drinking water yet," said Is'godt slapping his hand away. The water hit Ash'tan in the face and he stood dripping and humiliated.

"Perhaps there is a spring on the island – a running source of water is always much safer and sweeter," suggested Ab'ril. Both he and Is'godt turned away to study the island, discussing whether or not they should go there.

Still annoyed Ash'tan took a step forward his fist clenched, determined to take Is'godt down a peg or two.

Just who did he think he was throwing his weight around like that?

He've saw his intent and stopped him before he could achieve his aim.

"He means well," she whispered taking his hand. He threw away her hand and made a great show of taking a drink anyway, his defiant air warding off all further attempts at communication. Ignoring him she cocked her head to one side and listen instead to their conversation. They still seemed undecided.

"Please let us go, Is'godt. There may be food and fresh water. I have a good feeling about this," pleaded He've.

"You forget that we already have food. Perfectly good food," replied Is'godt. "There may be none at all over there or what we do find might be poisonous."

"I disagree. Anything is better than this," Ash'tan hissed holding up the snakeskin parcels of dried meat. He shuddered at the recollection of the desiccated smoky flavoured flesh between his teeth.

That was the last straw for Is'godt. He had gone too far this time.

"How dare you disdain the food that our mother worked hard to give us?" he shouted turning on him angrily. "You ungrateful whelp! If it wasn't for her you would have died along with your own mother. But out of the goodness of her heart she cared for you and treated you as her own."

The others could hardly believe their ears. Up until now no one had ever broken the unspoken rule by mentioning the other wife who had borne Ash'tan then died. They were afraid as to what it might mean. Another link to their past was now severed. It did not feel good at all. Is'godt had unwittingly flouted the law of their mother in her defence. If that was now abolished, what else were they going to lose?

He've had a good idea. She could see the division forming before her very eyes.

"Is'godt! He didn't mean it that way!" cried He've. "How could you?"

Ash'tan turned and fled, wading through the water till it was up to his waist then striking out to the island with a powerful front crawl stroke.

"Ash'tan! Come back!" He've called out after him. But she was wasting her breath.

The others turned expectantly to their leader who shrugged his shoulders apathetically.

"What did you expect me to do? He treated our mother with disrespect and he was trying to get us to go to the island even though I'd already decided against it. He is nothing more than a snake in the grass. We are better off without him."

"We cannot leave him. He is our brother – the blood of our father runs in his veins also," protested Ab'ril.

Still Is'godt remained unmoved.

"Please!" pleaded He've pulling at his arm. He shoved her away and she fell back into the water.

"Is'godt! Can't you see that this is dividing us when we need to stand together?" Ab'ril remonstrated. "There will always be differences of opinion between people - even family. Difference does not have to tear us apart. Our own mother chose to accept him for the sake of our family. She would be upset to know that you are acting like this."

His words struck home. In the end his mother's opinion carried that much weight.

"Alright," he said finally. "We will look for him. But you must be sure to stick together. We don't want to lose anyone else."

The others felt reassured by this last comment. Obediently they followed his lead as he ploughed through the water in pursuit of Ash'tan.

Once they made it to the sandy shore they called his name at the top of their voices.

"Ash'tan! Ash'tan!"

Perhaps he could not hear or perhaps he did not want to. Either way there was no reply.

"What do we do now?" they asked Is'godt.

Satisfied that once again they were looking to him for leadership he pushed aside the embers of his tantrum and sent them off to look for Ash'tan. While they searched one side of the island he boldly set out to search the other.

As the island was not that big it was not long before they came across him. They found him swimming happy and naked at the base of a small waterfall. They waved in greeting, smiling and relieved to have found him unharmed.

"What are you doing down there?" called He've raising her voice to be heard over the din of the waterfall. They parted the ferns in order to make their way down to him.

"I'm pleasing myself for a change, that's what," he called,

flipping over onto his back. "I'm tired of Is'godt bossing me around."

"I know he can come across that way sometimes," said He've. "But he does it because he cares. He's only trying to protect us."

"Oh really? He has a funny way of showing it. I think he made it quite clear back there that he couldn't care less about me. But who cares? I'm done with following orders."

"There you are!" called a voice from above. "We've been looking all over for you! Look out beloooow....!!!"

Suddenly, Is'godt appeared and launched himself into the air landing with a huge splash in the pool beside Ash'tan. His half-brother was both astonished and drenched. He came up spluttering for air.

He've and Ab'ril laughed loudly clapping their hands. They were happy to see that their leader was loosening up a little. Given time they believed everything would work out.

"So can we drink this water?" He've asked craftily.

"Ash'tan's approval is good enough for me," he said surprising them all by opening his mouth and taking a huge gulp. Before long they were all swimming, splashing and drinking, enjoying themselves as children should. They'd been serious for far too long.

But what had prompted this sudden alteration in Is'godt's mood Ash'tan wondered? All was soon to become clear.

"Now that you have drank your fill and washed away your cares, I want to show you a discovery that I have made," Is'godt told them.

It sounded intriguing. As he spoke Ash'tan thought he

caught a whiff of something intoxicatingly rich and fruity on his breath. He thought he recognised it but perhaps he was mistaken. Most likely it was the flowers growing at the foot of the waterfall.
As the others followed Is'godt with childlike eagerness Ash'tan's curiosity began to whittle away at him.

What was that unusual smell he had detected? He felt sure it had come from his half-brother. Suddenly the others came to an abrupt stop. Standing in front of them Is'godt spread out his arms in order to block their way.

Whatever he had to show them, he was making quite a song and dance about it.

"Ready?" he asked. They nodded and he drew back the heavy curtain of vines hanging between them and a large cleft in the rock. Before them was a tunnel with a light at the other end. Is'godt lead the way, enigmatic and silent. His sister He've followed close behind wondering at the warmth of the gentle breeze that flowed through the tunnel. Where was he taking them?

Suddenly, they left the corridor of rock and came out into the blinding light, stumbling over one another in the process. Once their eyes had adjusted they looked around completely awestruck.
Before them was more food than they could possibly eat in a month! Tree after tree was loaded down with Rinka fruit, Pajamin berries, Molaberries, Qortanuts, liareens, Chemons and many more.

It was just an amazing sight and it went a long way to explaining the smell of Is'godt's breath and his unusually good humour.

The children ran through the garden come orchard gorging themselves till late afternoon. When they'd eaten their fill they went in search of Is'godt whom they found staring at the most diseased, sickly looking tree they had ever set eyes upon. He seemed to be struggling with the urge to touch it. It was all very strange.

"Perhaps it's supposed to look like that," said He've coming up behind him to inspect the peculiar looking tree.

She covered her nose in disgust. It only had a few fruits on it which had to be said looked extremely unappetising. They were wrinkly brown and smelt like a cross between putrid flesh and wolverine dung. Yet somehow the longer she stood there the more desirable they seemed.

"He've! Do not touch those!" warned Is'godt grabbing her by the arm. Without even realising it she had been inching closer and closer to the tree as though drawn by magic. She froze – her arm poised outwards, stretching out to take what had to be the ugliest fruit known to man.

She swallowed hard, unsure of what had just happened.

"Is it poisonous?" she said as Is'godt led her away firmly. He wanted to put as much distance between her and the tree as possible.

"I don't know," he said truthfully. "But you must not touch it, else you may die. Stick to the trees and plants that we know. There is no need to touch anything else."

Filled with renewed respect after his discovery they all agreed to abide by this one rule. It did not seem like too much to ask for there were plenty of other things to eat and the power of its attraction had lessened now that they were a bit further away.

"This place is amazing," breathed He've when they had found somewhere to settle for the night. She was lying on her back looking up at the bright stars through the gaps in the forest canopy.

"How did you find it?" she asked Is'godt.

"I was out looking for Ash'tan just like you when I decided to follow my senses. They brought me here - to Eden."

"Eden?" the rest all said in unison.

"Yes. That is what I call this place – in honour of our mother."

"It has her beauty, that's for sure," said He've softly. "I want to stay forever."

"That would be unwise. I think we should leave in the morning," Is'godt said quietly.

"What?" Ab'ril cried in dismay. "Why?"

"I just know that this place spells trouble for us – I can feel it."

The others tried to talk him out of it but he would not be swayed. One by one they fell asleep feeling disjointed and alienated from each other and all they had ever known.

In the early hours of the morning when He've awoke she lay listen to the reassuring sound of her brothers breathing. In and out, in and out. Sigh, murmur, grumble. She smiled at the timeless familiarity of it all and found that it healed the wounds of their disagreement just a few hours before. Eventually she realised that something was not quite right. Someone was missing.

She turned over and saw in the greyish light of the coming dawn that Is'godt was gone. Surely he had not abandoned them?

Her heart beat a brisk tattoo as she left the group in search their leader. Hopefully he had just gone off somewhere to ease nature. Maybe he'd eaten too much fruit.

Without even knowing how she found herself at the foot of the ugly tree, looking up at its strange pendulous fruit.

"I thought I'd find you here." a voice said making her jump.

Ash'tan her half-brother had followed her.

"Go ahead," he hissed. "Take the fruit. I won't tell."

"Shhh!" she said looking round fearfully. "We're not supposed to."

"So why are you here then?"

She did not have an answer. Instead she had a question.

"Where do you suppose it came from? None of us have ever heard tell of this place – not even in legend."

"It hatched from the firebirds egg," Ash'tan said gravely. "It is no coincidence that we saw it fall from the sky the night before we stumbled across this place, which is why I think Is'godt is making a big mistake in deciding that we cannot stay. He himself said that the firebird brings our people good fortune. And here it is! We found food and water – enough to keep an entire tribe happy for a year or more."

"You're right!" He've declared a bit too loudly.

"Shhh!" whispered Ash'tan. "We should let Is'godt get his rest. Perhaps he will make better decisions then."

His half-sister nodded, forgetting that he was not asleep.

"You know, maybe he is wrong about this fruit business," she said.

"How do you mean?"

"Well if he's wrong about the Garden of Eden how can we be sure he's not wrong about this fruit?"

"We don't. All I know is that I'd much sooner make my own decisions for good or for bad. But that's just me."

Standing beneath the source of temptation He've weighed up the pros and cons. The longer she looked the more she wanted the freedom to choose for herself and to taste the forbidden fruit.

She could almost feel its juice running down her chin. She licked her lips then attempted to climb up Ash'tan's torso.

"Boost me up," she ordered.

Ash'tan smiled at her, glad that she was taking charge for once. Too long she'd been treated as if she was of no account. He held onto her ankles as she stretched up to reach her prize.

"Got it!" she said triumphantly and he set her back down on the ground.

"Eat!" he urged with a wicked grin.

For a moment she looked at it doubtfully.

"He've," he admonished. "It's bound to be good. It came from the firebird. It will bring you good fortune and long life. I want you to have this. You deserve it. You were the one who reached up and picked it. It belongs to you."

She felt touched by his words. She knew that he loved her and that he wanted what was best for her. Taking a deep breath she focused on that feeling of trust and took a huge bite from the ugly, forbidden fruit.

At first she chewed it slowly, savouring its unusual taste and texture. It was spicy and sticky sweet, with an overpowering taste of something she was at a loss to identify. That unidentified something was the bite of twenty six per cent alcohol mixed with formidable evolutionary accelerants.

A sense of elation jolted through her, coursing through her veins, making her feel supremely alive. She was suddenly so much more aware of her surroundings. She could even hear the noise the flamingos were making in the back of their throats and the steady thump, thump beat of Ash'stan's heart as he stood beside her. Not wanting to be selfish she made to share the strange fruit with him but he refused.

"I already tried it," he said with a secretive smile. Apparently the waterfall was his second stop after reaching the island. The Garden of Eden had been his first. She felt a bit shocked at his deceit.

"He've! What are you doing here?" asked a voice. Fearing it was Is'godt Ash'tan hid behind the thick trunk of the tree.

"It's ok," she told Ab'ril. "The fruit is not poisonous after all. It's very very good."

He approached her cautiously and watched her take another bite. It was not like her to be so rebellious, he thought.

"Here. Try it for yourself," she said offering him what was left.

There were only two bites left and that whetted his appetite so much for its strange taste that he resorted to eating the core and pips and all.

Seeing that there was nothing left on the tree, they were all over come by guilt. With surprising stealth they returned to the place where they had camped overnight in the hope that they hadn't been missed. Is'godt found them hours later when he reverted back to his human form. They were sticky with fruit and fast asleep. Having watched them from the fifth dimension, or what would later become known as the spirit realm, he knew exactly what had happened.

The three so called forbidden fruit that he had already eaten had endowed him with enough telepathic awareness to know that Ash'tan had tricked all of them. Although he was their half-brother he knew he could never be trusted again. He had used the powers he had gained from eating two of the fruit to encourage He've to disobey Is'godt. The power they derived from the fruit seemed to be transferable and could be exercised over others who were within reasonable proximity. Is'godt knew from his thought patterns that such power thrilled him and that if given the chance he would only abuse it. After all he'd already done so with his own flesh and blood.

Is'godt could not allow him to lead. For a start, Eden, his mother had prohibited it. His own actions had also proved it. His course was clear. Quickly he made his way down to the shore where he had hidden three more of the unique fruit between a group of rocks. He wolfed them down with the kind of haste and greed that would have earned him a slap from his mother, throwing the cores as far out into the water as he could.

He sat on the sand shaking and glowing silvery white with the sheer volume of power he now contained. It pulsated and grew by the second until there was nowhere left for it to go and no way for him to contain it.

Is'godt looked up at the glorious sun and held out his hand before leaving the human plain of existence forever.

Chapter Twenty Nine

Growth

BACK IN THE Oort Cloud God sat thinking about that time. He had not given it much thought lately. He remembered how he had felt when he had used his power to remove all traces of earthly experience from his sibling's memories. He hated to do it but it really was the only way. With their memories left intact they would never be able to give him the degree of respect he deserved – their humble origins would see to that.

Upon waking them he introduced himself as God, their creator, and gave them all new names. Ab'ril became Gabriel. Ash'tan became Satan and He've became He'vernon.

At first they were at a loss as to what to do but there was much to explore in the universe. Although this kept them extremely busy and God made sure to keep a close eye on Eden their mother – even going as far as keep her alive for much longer than all the other humans that had ever lived before her.

Eventually this became an impossible task. At the age of three hundred and six her body finally gave out and was placed on top of a limestone slab in a secondary chamber to the tribal cave. Heartbroken by her passing God decided to bring her to reside with them in the fifth realm or Heaven as it was now known.

But once in Heaven she pined over the loss of the life she had once known. She had no idea that she was surrounded by her sons and daughter and they themselves could not tell her. Seeing his mother so disheartened God decided to have some members of her family and tribe join her – most of them were nearing the end of their natural lives anyway. This made a big difference.

For many centuries God enjoyed her company and fondly watched the progress of his former tribe until one day a much bigger and more aggressive tribe ruled by a powerful king, came along and wiped them all out just because they desired their territory.

He felt completely outraged on their behalf to the point where even though he'd bought them all to the spirit realm he felt that something really ought to be done to punish the perpetrators. They had shown no mercy at all, not even to the old or young. The four siblings discussed what to do about it between themselves, which was of course how Hell eventually came into being and how their ethos eventually became focused on acting for the greater good of the human race – like caretakers from a distance.

All that was so many, many thousands of years ago, that if it wasn't for God's super human power he would never have been able to recall it at all. But there it was. That was the secret of the Ison Comet.

It was so special and unique that just one small chunk splitting off and falling to earth had created a mini ecosystem inside a crater practically overnight. The combination of unusual energies and evolutionary accelerators had changed the DNA structure of the plants and trees – especially one in particular.

When they ate the fruit from that tree it had flung the children forward millions of years along the evolutionary scale to the point where humans would no longer need bodies. All that remained was their energy and their consciousness, and that *was* considerable.

It had been so long since he had seen Ison and he'd been so busy with other things that he'd practically forgotten all about it. So when he saw some news item buzzing with talk of this newly discovered comet he'd panicked just a little.

Before he could do anything about it the Chinese had sent a probe. By then all he could do was falsify the results it sent back in the hope they would not realize its extraordinary powers.

That had gone well up until the comet exploded and split into three pieces. But this time the humans had his full attention like a thorn stuck in his proverbial side. They would not be getting their primitive little hands on his comet today or any other day. Not if he could help it.

Chapter Thirty

Snap Dragon

ON EITHER SIDE of the globe two government space agencies were racing against the clock to launch sophisticated probes that would intercept with the comet Ison. Both sides had fed each other false information through moles within their organizations about the timing and the true nature of what they intended to do.

Back in his heavenly office God sat at his heavy teak desk glued to the newsfeeds that were trained on unfolding events. Although he basically knew what was going to happen this time he still felt nervous. Humans were a lot more complicated than physics and this situation had a heady mixture of both components.

His secretary knocked on door to announce that he had visitors.

"I thought I told you not to disturb me?" he snapped.

"You did," she agreed. "But you also told me to inform you the moment Casey and Sarah returned."

He'd forgotten that they were missing what with all that was going on.

"Tell them to come back in an hour," he said. "And make sure they know that's an order. I don't want them disappearing again."

As she turned away he knew she rolled her eyes but he was far too busy to bother about that. In the corner of the screen two countdowns were in progress. He watched with interest wondering if he should have a cigar to calm his nerves. That would mean taking his eye off the situation though which was a risk he wasn't willing to take.

Angry shouting suddenly arose outside. It sounded like Casey but he was far too interested in watching the tiny humans scurrying around the separate launch pads. There was only one more minute remaining.

He gripped his arm rests and leaned forward as though it might help him see better. It had been a long time since anything had grabbed his interest to this extent.

Ten, nine, eight, seven, six, five, four, three, two, one. Orange flames shot out from the launch pad signalling that they had lift off. Without looking he felt around behind him for the cigar box on the desk. It was too much. He had to have one.

With a flick of his solid gold lighter the end of it glowed brightly as he took a long blissful drag. He sat back in his chair and watched the two blazing probes making their merry way towards Ison.

Back in NASA headquarters Martin Stewart and Austin Matner both looked at the screen in dismay.

"What do you mean, they're going to collide?" growled the national security advisor. He was talking to Martin, the director of

NASA, through his ear piece.

"I don't know what to tell you, sir. Our intel must have been wrong. I've ran through our calculations multiple times. There is nothing wrong with them. They're perfect."

"I see. Is there no way to alter the trajectory?"

"I'm afraid not sir," said the director swallowing painfully. "Well it's a good job we decided not to man the probe after all then. I suppose all that's left now then is for us sit back and watch the most expensive firework display in history," he said curtly.

"I guess so," agreed Martin.

The line went dead and Martin flopped into the nearest chair. The room suddenly exploded with chatter as his team tried to make sense of what had happened.

Half an hour later Austin took himself off to the restrooms and locked himself inside a cubicle. Once he'd settled himself comfortably on the toilet lid he pulled a miniaturized Apple Mac from inside his jacket. Hastily, he booted up and connected to the live feed from the two probes.

Good! He wasn't too late.

They were still a few seconds away from disaster. He held his breath hardly daring to watch. Then all of a sudden, just as they had predicted…BOOM! Or else it would have been if it were possible for sound to carry in space.

He leapt up off the toilet seat and punched the air repeatedly in triumph.

"Yes!" he yelled. "THANK God!"

When he put away his apple mac and came out of the toilet cubicle he got the shock of his life. All that time he thought he'd been alone in there one of the students had been standing by the mirror quietly dabbing at a nose bleed. Only a true hypochondriac would have missed that over something so minor thought Austin.

As he washed his hands their eyes met briefly in the mirror.

"You ok buddy?" he said.

"No," replied the hypochondriac with a shake of his head. "I thought this was just a nose bleed but now I'm wondering if it isn't something much more serious."

Austin peered at him in concern.

"Oh? Like what?"

"Could be a brain tumour. I hear you can get nose bleeds and auditory hallucinations with that."

"So you've been hearing stuff?"

"Yes."

"Like what?"

"Well just now, I thought I heard you talking to God in the bathroom stall and everyone knows you would never do that."

"Too right I wouldn't. Maybe it wouldn't be a bad thing if you got checked out at medical?" replied Austin feigning concern.

"Oh really? You think so?"

"Yes I do. Tell them I sent you."

"I will. Thank you for your concern."

"Don't mention it," said Austin exiting the restroom. He paused briefly outside the door feeling thoroughly and utterly ashamed of himself.

If there is a Hell I'm going there, he thought.

Chapter Thirty One

Mirror Me Magic

THE MOMENT THE debris had cleared from the explosion and the comet was out of danger God reached out with his power and triggered yet another explosion.

Rather than being a destructive force its objective was to mask what he was really doing. Behind the shield of its fury God tinkered with the comets make up all the way down to the sub atomic level. From where he sat in his office he carefully directed the matter of the newborn comet he had found in the Oort Cloud and exchanged it via a dimensional tear in space for that which made up the comet Ison.

It was all very complicated and stressful but thankfully it only took a split second.

There was precision involved which was more than just the timing. It had to be a good match too. Which was why he had had to go to the Oort Cloud physically – to be sure that apart from the evolutionary accelerants and the unnamed element that had given him his special powers, that the two comets were absolutely identical. No one would know the difference – even he couldn't tell from this distance.

Now all that remained was to find somewhere to stash Ison for safe keeping. The heart of the sun seemed like the most logical place. It would be a long time until humans had the capability to go there and they'd be much too busy chasing after the precious elements they'd discovered in the Oort cloud now. It would make an excellent distraction from what he had done even if it did spark off the odd war or two.

In the blink of an eye he'd cast it into that celestial blast furnace where he watched it sink down until it became lost in its depths. He turned away, satisfied that it was safe for the time being. All he had to do now was remember where he'd put it and get on with running the Universe.

It probably wouldn't be long before things got boring again, he thought glumly.

Chapter Thirty Two

AWOL

"GOD WILL SEE you now," said the receptionist sitting filing her nails at the desk.

Casey helped Sarah to her feet, his anger rising once again at the sight of her tear stained face.

"Ah there you are!" God said when they walked in. "I was beginning to wonder where you two had got to."

Casey frowned. He had expected him to be angry with them for going AWOL. It appeared he had barely noticed their absence.

"Ok. Perhaps you'd better start at the beginning. Give me a brief rundown of what happened and what you've been up to."

He pulled out his tablet from the drawer in his desk and as Casey spoke he started to type.

As Casey got to the part where Fernando's men had killed Carlos God let out an almighty laugh. Sarah and Casey were deeply shocked.

"I'm sorry," he said. "That was bad timing. I was just updating my MYSPIRIT status when I saw a funny comment that

Gabriel had posted."

"If this is more important we can come back later," said Casey in an odd voice. He had thought initially that God had been taking notes.

"Don't be silly!" he said setting down the tablet. "Please continue."

Before Casey could open his mouth Sarah beat him to it.

"They killed him! Don't you understand? They killed him!" she sobbed.

"And now we don't know where he is," Casey added.

God scratched his head absently.

"Have you checked the records?"

"Yes."

"And he's not in heaven?"

"No," Casey answered putting his arm round Sarah.

"Well then there's only one place left that he can be," God told them.

"No," said Sarah shaking her head in disbelief. "No. Not there! He's a good man. He doesn't belong there!"

"Can't you do something?" Casey asked.

"I'm sorry. Hell is Satan's domain. I tend not to interfere. And besides - he took someone's life. I'm not sure those are the actions of a good man."

Sarah sobbed uncontrollably.

"No! They are the actions of a wonderful man who through no fault of his own has been messed up by all the crap going on in the world around him!"

"I see you have developed quite an attachment there," God observed dryly. "This is why we have rules against consorting with humankind. It never works out. Their limitations are too great."

"I must say that you have proved to be quite the exception though," he added turning to Casey now. "When your predecessor nominated you as the next Karma we thought it would never work. It just seemed crazy! Your character was deemed irreformable by the vast majority. But I can honestly say that I am both pleased and pleasantly surprised that you have been able to prove us wrong on that count. And your last mission to extend good Karma to someone deserving has been a success also. I'm sure Sarah greatly appreciates the chance you gave her to say her goodbyes to Carlos before he died. It was an excellent way to thank her for all her hard work in training you. Don't you agree Sarah?"

She looked vaguely confused but nodded anyway. Casey stared blankly at the desk. He was beginning to see what was happening here. God was assuming that he intended Sarah to be the recipient of his first good Karma ruling. He thought that Casey had taken her to earth to make peace with the fact that Carlos, the love of her life was to die and end up in Hell. No wonder God thought he was clever and extremely well suited to his role.

Determined to prove at least the first part of that statement true Casey decided to take a gamble in the hope that he could put everything right. It was a long shot but it just might work.

"So I have completed my training now?" he said hopefully.

"Yes. And with flying colours no less! All that remains now is to make the announcement."

He clicked his fingers and a web cam appeared in mid-air. It's lens trained itself automatically on the three of them.

"Could you step out of shot for just a moment there Sarah? Thank you."

Sarah stepped aside and God began the announcement. "Citizens of the fifth realm, I have a special announcement to make – one that concerns every being in the Universe whether they are aware of it or not."

Casey's scalp prickled. There! That was the confirmation he needed. His nerves were stretched taut like the strings of a freshly tuned violin.

"Today we must welcome a new and unusual addition to our ranks – Casey Davenport has passed his training and will now take over the role of Karma with all the power that that entails."

There was a deafening round of applause as God leaned forward and pressed his thumb to Casey's forehead conferring upon him the entire sum of Karma's power. Somewhere in Hell, Cal his father watched with pride as all its inhabitants had temporarily been released from their torments.

"Well done son," he whispered still smoking from his early morning dip in the lake of sulphur.

"You must be proud," said the South American priest standing beside him.

"Yes, I am."

Casey turned to smile as he shook God's hand and the webcam shut itself off thereby ending the transmission. Still distraught Sarah snuck out unnoticed to offload her cargo of tears in private.

"May I offer you a cigar?" God said opening up the drawer that housed his precious tobacciana collection.

"Don't mind if I do," Casey said dipping his hand in to retrieve an expensive Cuban cigar. They leaned back in their chairs and puffed out clouds of smoke in the direction of the ceiling.

Casey looked calm but inside he was a bundle of nerves.

"So have you any thoughts as to who you might choose for your first case?" God asked. He lifted up his tablet once more and scrolled down the page with a smile. "I see some of the guys are already placing bets as to who it will be."

"Oh I don't think the person I've chosen will be on that list."

God threw his head back and laughed.

"Now why doesn't that surprise me?" he said. "You always were one for thinking outside the box."

Casey made no comment.

"Well come on. Who is it?" God asked. "The suspense is killing me here."

"You," said Casey softly.

His cigar fell from his lips into his lap.

"WHAT?"

"You heard me. I choose you. No one in Heaven, Hell or Earth needs it more than you."

"You do know that I could quite easily blast you to atoms?" God said angrily.

"Go right ahead. I've got nothing to lose. But I strongly doubt that you will do that. You just told the entire spirit realm that you have approved me as Karma and besides…we're live on air," said Casey pointing to the floating webcam. He'd restarted it using his new found powers.

Throughout Heaven and Hell a collective gasp rang out. What was he going to do next? Die, most likely he thought with a pang.

"What are the charges? On what do you base this

outrageous decision?" demanded God.

"They are many and varied."

God flushed a devilish shade of scarlet.

"Perhaps we should take this to court then," he said haughtily.

"My thought, precisely," said Casey almost swallowing his heart with anxiety.

Chapter Thirty Three

Finally It Hits the Fan

FOR A PLACE with so many assembled the Arena of Time was curiously quiet. No one dared so much as rustle their wings while they waited for the Almighty to take his seat.

In the centre stood a very overwhelmed looking Gabriel whose job it was to preside over the trial. Directly in front of the bench He'vernon had been charged with recording the proceedings. Such a situation was unprecedented. God was the only one who had ever addressed them here. To say they felt disloyal didn't even come close. They were scared witless.

"We are gathered here today to hear the case of Karma versus God. If you would, please approach the bench and state the nature of your grievances Karma," Gabriel commanded.

Casey stood to address the courtroom.

"Firstly I would like to get one thing straight before we go any further," he said wishing his knees would stop shaking. "I personally, do not have any problem with God as an individual. In any dealings that we have had he has always treated me reasonably.

Before I came to heaven I never even believed in God. I am more than happy to be proved wrong. The concept of a higher power who acts as a benefactor towards the human race is a wonderful one – alas the reality itself I find is a little more flawed."

Everyone seemed happy enough with his initial statements so he moved in to drop the bomb shell.

"The accusations I bring against God today are as follows; he has knowingly and willingly allowed human beings as well as the rest of the Universe to be misled about his true nature in some cases to their detriment. He has on numerous occasions displayed a level of selfishness that has put even me to shame. And finally, he is responsible for the death of hundreds of thousands if not millions of human beings."

Shock reverberated around the courtroom.

When Gabriel finally recovered he asked Karma to bring his first witness.

"Please state your name for the record."

"Sarah."

"Thank you," Karma said patting her arm.

"Sarah, can you tell me a little bit about yourself – about your life before you came to heaven?"

She nodded and went onto explain how she had been born blind and that her parents had arranged for her to be brought up in a convent. There she had learnt about God and what it means to be one of his children.

"You were very zealous – a faithful woman by all accounts. It says here that you cared for the elderly, sick and helped out at the orphanage. That must not have been easy for someone who was blind. I understand too that you made many sacrifices along the way. Most notably in love."

Sarah looked embarrassed but instead of denying it she nodded.

"You did your best to refrain from forming a relationship with a priest who you were strongly attracted to as you both wanted to serve God without distraction. Is this correct?"

"Yes," said Sarah. Tears formed in her eyes and she wiped them away with the back of her hand.

"And how did God reward you for this devotion? How did you end up in heaven?"

"I got hit by lightning one day whilst out walking."

"Really? The odds of that happening are extremely slim. It's like winning the worst lottery ever! But I'm sure that God had good reason for letting this happen or maybe even causing this to happen. Did you ever ask him?"

"No."

"No?" echoed Karma looking round the court. "Well I think that maybe you should. Go head. Ask him. Ask him why he allowed a blind woman who was fiercely loyal to him to be hit by lightning."

For a moment or two Sarah said nothing. She just looked at her knees and fidgeted. Eventually she found the courage and asked the burning question.

"Why?"

God coughed and blustered.

"All you need to know is that it was part of my purpose."

"Sounds a lot like that old cherry 'it was God's will'," said Karma. "You're going to have to do better than that. How did killing a blind woman fit in with your purpose?"

"Look," said God. "You know how these religious people can be and the kind of stuff that they respond to. Let's just say that you have to kill off a couple of the really devout ones every now and then to kick them into a higher gear and leave it at that. Keep them on their toes as it were."

There was a commotion in the Arena as those gathered assimilated this information. They had no idea that this was God's policy. Many of them had been devout people back on earth so it was quite likely that this is exactly what had befallen them. God sensed that the wave of public opinion had turned in favour of Karma.

"It's for the greater good!" he protested. They did not look convinced.

"If that was the case wouldn't the world be a better place?" Karma said pointedly. "I call to the stand my next witness."

"State your name for the court record please. Don't be scared."

At Karma's encouragement the little boy spoke loud and clear.

"My name is Ricardo."

"Ricardo, could you tell us about yourself and how you came to be in Heaven?"

Ricardo explained in his sweet lilting voice how he and his sister Maria were street children from Mexico City where they were constantly abused and harassed.

"We saw many of our friends die," he said matter of fact. "How - if you don't mind my asking? Did they die of starvation?"

"No. They were murdered just like Maria and I."

Karma remembered finding Maria's dead body beside

Fernando's. It was not a pleasant memory.

"I'm sorry," he said simply.

"Before you go I have one last question. Did you at any time ask for God's help? Did you pray?"

"Many times – just ask Father Ramirez over there. He prayed with me," the little boy pointed him out in the audience. Carlos had been allowed out of Hell on day release under the pretext that Karma may need him to testify.

"So in this instance, not one but two people prayed to you for help – one of them deeply religious. Did you hear their pleas?" he asked the accused.

"Of course. I can hear all petitions directed to me," God answered.

"And yet you did nothing?"

"Like I told you before, I have to do what's best for the greater good. There's always a bigger picture. I cannot intervene in every little detail of people's lives. I tried that before with the Israelites and they hated it most of the time. They even killed the prophets I sent to teach them about me," God said.

"Yes I'm sure Ricardo here would have deeply resented you preventing his murder. Want to know what I think? I think the only big picture that you care about is your own. You've become far too self-absorbed to concern yourself with the daily affairs of man."

"That's not true," God replied. But he did not sound very convincing.

"So where were you when Ricardo and Maria were slain at the hand of Fernando?"

"I was busy!"

"Helping somebody else?"

"I had a personal matter to attend to."

"And of course that was far more important than the lives of two innocent children."

"On this occasion it was."

"So rather than help them, you sent me down there to make an example of their killer in the hope that it may make people more God fearing in the future. Am I right?"

"Yes."

"So once again, it's all about you isn't it?"

"Look! I'm not perfect! What do you want me to say?" God cried.

There was a gasp of horror from those assembled. This was news to them!

"And what about all the countless people that suffer and die from disease, murder and famine day after day? From what I know of you all this is eminently preventable. So I ask you, what court down on Earth would fail to convict a man who'd stood by and watched his own children be slain in such a manner? Yet this is what you do day in day out, century after century. Your inaction is what makes you culpable. You KNOW you could do more."

God sat motionless, staring out at the sea of faces before him. Karma had shown him in a very different light and thrown the whole assembly into turmoil. Ison had not destroyed him – Karma had.

"If you are to discharge your duties as Almighty God in a way that it both beneficial and merciful for the universal populace then you must never lose sight of what it is to be human. I hereby enforce a fifty per cent emotional link with all your subjects in order that you may never again deem any of their trials and tribulations as trivial or worse still beneath your notice. From now on, their problems will be your problems. Amen!"

Gabriel sealed the judgement with a harsh crash of his gavel.

Almost immediately God roared as though in terrible pain, shaking the very foundations of Heaven.

Everyone cowered as he fell to his knees. Some of them covered their faces. What had Karma done? Everyone craned forward to see. Suddenly a hand shot up and grabbed the bench for support. Gasping and dazed God pulled himself up bodily until he was back on his own two feet. He drew himself up to his full height and pointed a glowing finger at Karma. Everyone held their breath.

"YOU...did well," he said. "I know of no one else who would have had the guts to do what you just did. But it was necessary. I can feel the pain and fears of everyone now. I admit that it is not...it is not at all pleasant. That pain will move me to act in ways that I have no done so before. And for that I thank you Karma."

Casey bowed his head in respect. The outcome was more than he could have hoped for. He'd survived to tell the tale and more! Yet there was one thing left that he still had to do...

"Everyone here knows I had a big debt to repay. I hope that this has reduced it a little."

God nodded.

"As much as I appreciate all the effort that Sarah put into training me I have finally decided this life is not for me," he said sadly. "I hereby relinquish my role of Karma and recommend Carlos Ramirez for the position. He has already shown himself capable but I am sure that Sarah will not mind taking him under her wing until he is ready to stand alone."

He winked at Sarah who was sitting crying in the gallery. Thank you, she mouthed.

"But what about you? Surely you don't want to live out the rest of your sentence locked in a body that's withering away?" God said.

"Whatever will be, will be," said Casey shaking his hand. "I am more at peace now than I ever was. My awareness that there is something greater than suffering has healed me. I thank you Father."

Chapter Thirty Four

Take Two

RIGHT ON TIME a big black cloud formed over the city soaking the inhabitants to the skin. A woman and her toddler rushed through the streets in a desperate bid to reach the bus stop. If they missed the last bus they'd have to walk eight blocks in the rain to get to their tiny apartment over on west side.

The child in the buggy thought it was all a delightful game and shrieked with delight at her mother's mad pace.

Life however had taught her mother to be a little more cautious. She did not want her child to catch pneumonia. She was all Valentina had now that she was estranged from her mother. From her position in the heavens He'vernon smiled as she squeezed out every last drop from the rain cloud. This time her actions really were for the greater good.

As the young mother charged round the corner scattering pedestrians and vendors every which way she saw the bus overtake her from the corner of her eye. She waved frantically hoping that it might stop but it didn't. This was Detroit for heaven's sake!

Seeing her disappointment Casey moved in. He'd been sitting on a crowded bench squashed between two incontinent old ladies, waiting for Valentina to appear. Difficult as it was he'd been trying to get to grips with the new body he'd been given. This one was even taller than the last one – but God had suggested that it might make Valentina feel safe. She still carried a lot of baggage from the attack. From the heavenly realm above Gabriel did his thing and halted time in order to give Casey chance to move into position and collect his wits. No one really did know how it was that he had that unique ability. God himself could not even replicate it. God suspected it was because he had eaten the pips and core of the forbidden fruit but there was no way to test that theory. Either way, it came in handy every now and then which wasn't such a bad thing.

"Are you ready?" God asked him, his voice echoing inside his mind.

"Yes," said Casey.

"Ok...well go meet your daughter," he said. "And behave yourself this time round..."

"I will."

"Good luck."

Gabriel restarted time and Casey rushed forward to stop the bus in order to allow Valentina on. He smiled as Casey even leant down to help her with the buggy. He'd come a long way from what he had been. But then again, so had God. His new found awareness of other peoples suffering would not allow him to send Casey back to Earth to be trapped inside a body that was slowly degenerating.

Instead he was giving him a second chance – a chance to begin again.

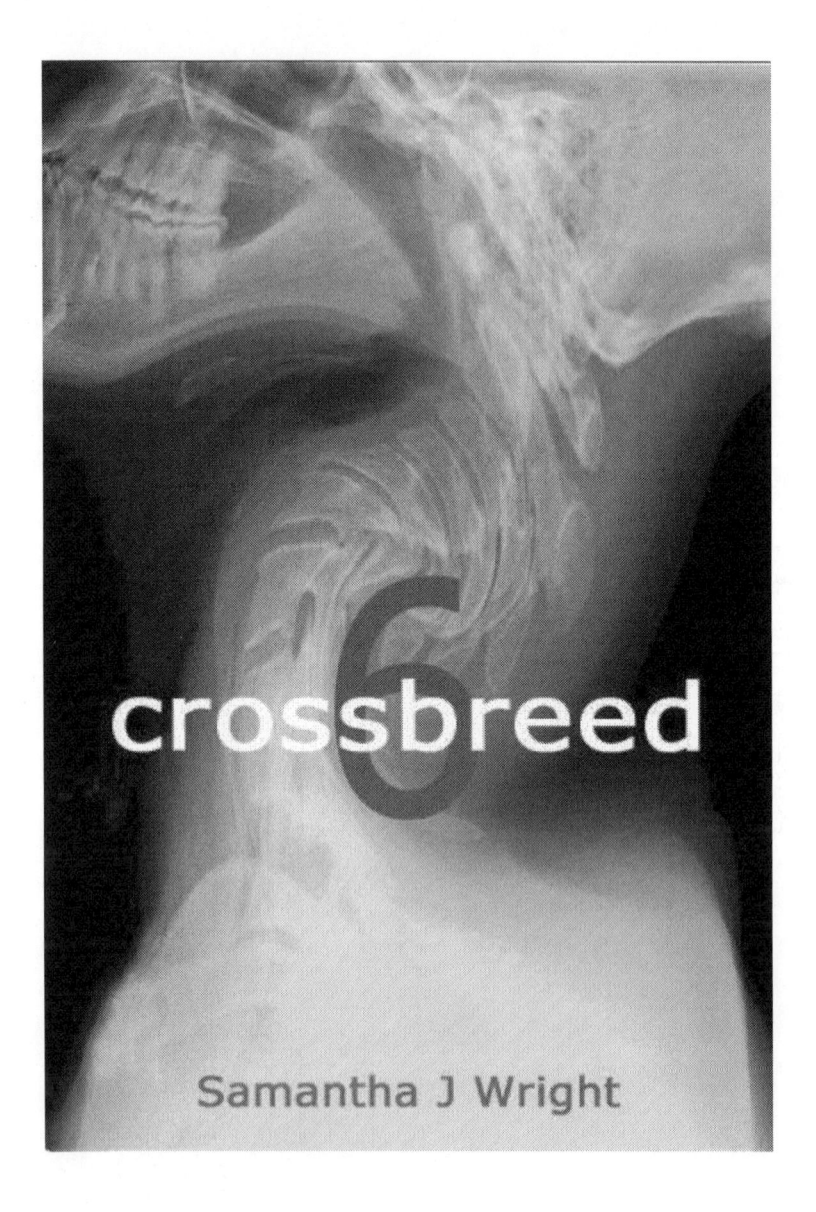

Also available by Samantha J Wright on Amazon worldwide

Crossbreed 6

A spicy selection of six short paranormal Syfy stories for all those curious fantasaical minds out there…

A Darker 6

A collection of flash fiction that delves into the realms of, what if? Supernatural powers, freaks of nature, alien life forms and alternate realities, you'll find them all here in this superb anthology.

ABOUT THE AUTHOR

Originally from Staffordshire, Samantha J Wright moved to Northern Ireland 18 years ago where she now lives with her two children. Although she has worked in other fields (such as retail and accountancy) and is training to be a counsellor, she has always had the urge to write and has done so for personal pleasure over the last few decades.

In 2010 she decided to have a real stab at writing something publishable which resulted in her first novel, **The Sands of Carsaig**. **Night Chorus** shortly followed (a sequel to the first) as well as a compilation of short stories all of which are available on Amazon. During her early teens she was an avid reader of the sci-fi genre with its many and varied subcategories. This stayed with her throughout adulthood but up until now has actually never filtered through to her novels. "To me sci-fi has a much greater scope for the imagination which holds unique appeal for me as both writer and reader. It made sense then that I should eventually go down this route and produce something which harked back to my earlier days of reading Arthur C Clarke and Isaac Asimov," she says.

"This and the transformation of my spirituality over the years combined with my avid interest in the newly discovered comet Ison spawned the seeds of my latest creation The Ison Delusion. It was such a joy to write that after completion I immediately started work on another sci-fi which as of yet is unnamed. Watch this space for details."

The last few years have not been easy in many respects. Issues in her personal life unfortunately had an impact on her ability to write – not least the death of her husband by suicide. "After a difficult and stressful time I've eventually found my buzz again and am eager to see what lies just over the horizon. Ideas are once again coming thick and fast and I am relieved to discover that the creative side of me has not been lost."

Made in the USA
Charleston, SC
30 May 2013